MW00905287

BLACK FRIDAY

TOM DICAPRIO

Order this book online at www.trafford.com
or email orders@trafford.com

Most Trafford titles are also available at major online book retailers.

Printed in the United States of America.

ISBN: 978-1-4669-9787-5 (sc)
ISBN: 978-1-4669-9788-2 (hc)
ISBN: 978-1-4669-9789-9 (e)

Library of Congress Control Number: 2013910214

Trafford rev. 10/01/2013

www.trafford.com

North America & international
toll-free: 1 888 232 4444 (USA & Canada)
fax: 812 355 4082

Friday November 23
12:00 a.m.

"How low is it supposed to go tonight?" Irene Daley asked her sister Irma.

"I heard that it was going down to twenty five." Irma Daley replied as the two twenty six year old twin sisters were waiting in the one hundred person long line for Target to open just three hours from now.

"I wonder if Dad's finally home." Irene mused in reference to Ian Daley returning from his job at Homeland Security.

"It had to be very serious for Dad to leave in the middle of Thanksgiving dinner." Irma noted.

"I couldn't agree with you more." Irene remarked as the twins were now freezing in the cold crisp night air. They were outside Target in The Suburban Mall. The popular strip mall was located in a suburb of Bethesda. Meanwhile the two slender 5'6" twins were sipping on their thermoses of French Vanilla coffee. They were bundled up wearing light blue and tan winter coats respectively. Their scarves and knit hats matched up. The two now saw more people get into the line. "I think we will be at two hundred people in line before we know it." The clear crisp night sky was illuminated by the countless stars which dominated the sky. The Target store was the centerpiece of The Suburban Mall which stretched in an L-shape that would take up a total of three NFL football fields. The parking lot would fit at least two thousand cars while it had enough room for a bus stop that would hold five commuter busses at any one time. Across the street of The Suburban Mall was known at "Tech Row." Tech Row was a series of technological businesses that were next to one another on Maryland Avenue. Several yards away behind The Suburban Mall as well as Tech Row were forests. The trees had been standing since the Meso-Colonial Period. Birds, deer, fox, raccoon, possum and insects resided in the forests to this day. The Bethesda area chapter of the National Wildlife Federation had been staging a series of protests periodically every time the developers of both The Suburban Mall and Tech Row desired to expand their respective businesses by proposing to mow down the forests that were behind them. Each time this was proposed it outraged the local as well as the regional conservation activists to the extent that the plan was ultimately abandoned after months of haggling. This made the residents of Hopkins, Maryland become emotionally numb whenever the proposals were made given the fact that they would never be passed into law.

"I take it you two are bored." a middle aged woman began "I've been through this ritual every year since 1987." Her tan overcoat and knit hat covered her lithe 5'0" frame. The platinum blonde with blue eyes continued "Believe me, you two will be a veteran at this like me someday." With that the Daley twins and the middle aged women began to have a lively conversation with one another.

"Unusual chatter coming from Afghanistan." Ian Daley began as he then added "Brings back memories of 9/11." The 5'9" sixty one year old veteran of the counterterrorism community with gray hair and green eyes as well as a medium build noted as he kept looking over the latest report. He was casually dressed in a blue button down denim shirt and tan khaki slacks with blue, brown and tan argyle socks and brown loafers.

"Come on Daley, we've seen this since 9/11." Art Graves replied. The 6'2" fifty year old grizzled data analyst began to roll his eyes as he then added "Remember that supposed threat two years ago. We thought for sure that something was going to happen, but we all know that nothing occurred. How about five years ago when . . ." Graves wore a tan sweater and brown dress pants along with tan shoes and dark brown socks.

"You've made your point!" Daley stated exasperatedly as he put his hands towards Graves. "What if we ignored the signs and we actually have another 9/11?"

"Do you really think that there will be another 9/11?" Art inquired with a quizzical look on his face.

"Look anything is possible. We must never rule out any scenario." Ian said.

"Whatever you say, but federal resources are being depleted by the day." Graves began as Daley cut him off "It is that same mindset that resulted in 9/11. Look we must never be complacent. Do I have to remind you what happened the last time we were complacent?" as an African American male walked over to the men and said "Briefing in Harrison's office ASAP!"

"Yes sir." they replied as they walked briskly to Harvey Harrison's office.

"Could you tell us what this is about?" Graves asked Reginald Patterson."

"Let's just say that it's urgent." Patterson noted. The 6'5" 220 pound former forward for the Washington Bullets was immaculately dressed in a gray suit, black shirt and a charcoal gray tie. His black socks and matching shoes as well as a receding pate which never went gray gave him an aura of self-confidence. His mustache matched his hair and his black glasses give him a dignified look. His voice had the inflection of an individual with an Ivy League pedigree. The complex which housed this particular branch of the Homeland Security department was in the middle of the complex of businesses in Washington, DC. However the complex was aptly named Ridgemont in honor of the first director of Homeland Security former Pennsylvania governor Tom Ridge who served less than one term during the first four years of the George W. Bush administration. Ridgemont was surrounded by a seven foot metal fence which made the peaks of the three story building visible. Outside the complex stood armed guards at the gate. They checked for ID each time someone would enter Ridgemont. Once they saw the identification card, the guards placed a call to a desk secretary who verifies if the person was supposed to be working on a particular shift or was summoned to work on an emergency basis. Once their identification was confirmed, they would proceed inside where their cars went through a rigorous security search. This is the reason that the employees of Ridgemont hardly kept anything inside their cars and kept it empty for the most part. Their identifications were then quickly vetted while they went through a series of metal detectors as well as body scans. After that they would be allowed to enter the main sections of the complex. The main sections of the complex actually looked like corporate offices with modern desks, furniture as well as art deco. The only exceptions were in the private rooms there were state of the art computers with the latest technology to track down terrorists as well as the latest terror threats that Ridgemont would receive every fifteen minutes.

It was now late morning inside the al-Qaeda camp in a mountainous area in Afghanistan. Five men were inside Ayman al-Zawahiri's tent. The al-Qaeda leader was holding court with his top lieutenants. They were going over planning for future operations. Now Omar Ali Mustafa inquired "How is Operation Yarmuk going?" in reference to the first battle against the Byzantine Empire which was led by Khalid Ibn al Walid. This very scenario mentioned in the book *Future Jihad* by Walid Phares.

"We have our agents in place and ready to strike at the given signal." al-Zawahiri replied.

"What is the signal?" Khalid Isawi asked. The higher up in the al-Qaeda hierarchy was 5'11" and 185 pounds. He wore a white turban and long multi-color flowing robes. His gray mustache and beard cover most of the olive skin on his face.

"Watch CNN today. You will find out soon enough." al-Zawahiri remarked. He then changed the subject "Do you have anything new to report about the trade?" he inquired in reference to the heroin fields that have been recently proliferating throughout Afghanistan that were primarily run by the Taliban, but were partnered up with al-Qaeda as well.

"There are four shipments that are on the way to America, Venezuela, Columbia as well as Mexico. We have operatives in each place of destination." Isawi replied.

"When do you think that the shipments will be arriving?" Ayman al-Zawahiri asked.

"Any day now." Isawi noted. Khalid Isawi for years had worked as a peasant farmer who was unable to make ends meet in a small village that was outside Jalalabad, Afghanistan. His life was basically a dead end road in which that he would realize that being essentially a migrant farmer who was basically serving a life sentence of poverty despite the fact that his family owned the farm and that as the middle child he would never be able to own the farm. Isawi was resigned not by choice to live a life in which he had no future until he first heard of al-Qaeda through a fiery sermon being given from one of the Imams at a mosque in the next town over rail about how the infidels were occupying Saudi Arabia. This would begin a series of a chain reaction of events that would forever change the life of Abdul Isawi. Isawi became not only a radical Moslem but also befriended the Imam who convinced Isawi to join al-Qaeda. Isawi left his family behind and made his way to the camp which was outside Kabul, Afghanistan. For the next few months, Isawi was not only trained with weapons, but with explosives as well until he first learned of the drug trade. He knew that there was a lot of money to be made by harvesting drug crops such as heroin and opium. Meanwhile his parents and two older brothers died due to a flu that raged its way throughout the Jalalabad area during the winter of 1997-1998. It was then that Abdul Isawi inherited the farm that he had toiled at without making enough money to live on. He immediately began to plant heroin as well as opium and practically overnight he went from living a life of poverty to one of opulence. Isawi overnight became the wealthiest person in the Jalalabad region and he never forgot how and when his fortunes began to change. He was known for making numerous donations to the mosque where he first converted to radical Islam, al-Qaeda as well as the Taliban. Isawi also had numerous customers who were drug lords in Latin American countries such as Mexico, Columbia and Venezuela. It was the drugs that were sold to those aforementioned drug lords that seeped its way into the United States and made millions of Americans into drug addicts. Their craving for those drugs resulted in more sales of the heroin crops from Afghanistan. It was the proceeds from the sale of drugs such as heroin and opium that were used to finance terrorist attacks against the

United States as well as other western nations and Israel. The drug business not only made Isawi very wealthy but the Taliban and al-Qaeda as well. As a result, al-Qaeda now had another income stream that would finance terrorist attacks globally. The plot that they are about to bring to fruition was financed by the drug trade.

"What is the status of your readiness to strike if needed?" Chang Huang Dong the commander of the Chinese military asked his commander of the 10th Chinese Fleet which was stationed off the southeastern Chinese coast. The 5'5" 140 pound sixty year old who was born in Beijing was a product of Mao's Cultural Revolution. His gray hair and piercing black eyes gave him an intimidating look about him. He was in much better physical condition than most of his military counterparts.

"My men are as ready as they will ever be." Sung Jin Liang replied "How soon would you like me to enact Operation Reunification?" The fellow Beijing native stood 5'6" and weighed 150 pounds. Although he was fifty five, he and Chang went back to their twenties when they served in the same battalion. Chang took Sung under his wing and the two would go on to advance in the chain of command in the Chinese military to such high levels.

"We have a spy who is well placed in the upper levels of the United States government." Chang began "We have reason to believe that such an operation may commence within the next twenty four hours."

"Very well then." Sung responded "When would you like me to inform my men to become battle ready?"

"They must be informed as soon as this meeting comes to an end." Chang ordered "Remember the pride of the Motherland hinges on how well we carry out this excursion. Dismissed."

Meanwhile at another meeting inside a nuclear facility in a secluded area in the central part in North Korea, the head of the North Korean Atomic Commission was meeting with the North Korean Defense Minister. Also present was the commander of the North Korean Military.

"Are the missiles ready for use?" Defense Minister Hung Su Kim asked the head of the North Korean Atomic Commission Jang Nuan Do.

"Yes." Jang began "An underground test of the Taepodong VII was successfully executed early this morning."

"We will need you to carry out a nuclear launch within the next twenty four hours." Hung ordered Jang who now looked not only shocked but had the look of someone who was about to realize his lifelong dream of striking South Korea and annexing it in the process. Meanwhile Hung noticed the look on Commander Kim Song Park who was about to ask a question. He then said to Kim "I know that you are about to ask about the American military presence at the 38th Parallel. We will use one of the bombs on them as well. Besides their government will not be able to respond to us anyways."

"How so?" Kim inquired.

"We have an agent inside the upper levels of the United States government. He has been working with us as well as the Chinese government in order to make sure that both our objectives are carried out successfully." Hung noted "First have the soldiers and the weapons ready and second we must wait for the events in the United States to take place. Trust me you will know when to carry out the operation."

"The recount has now entered its seventeenth day with no end in sight." the CNN reporter began "The Ohio, Pennsylvania, Florida, Arizona and West Virginia State Supreme Courts will be hearing arguments regarding the disputed votes. As it stands, President Jeff Wolcott will be updating the nation this afternoon on the latest in the crisis. Meanwhile his challenger Virginia Governor Dick Freeman has indicated that he will not back down on any challenges that he has made regarding the disputed votes." as the screen now showed the fifty one year old Freeman state for the record "I am no Al Gore. I will not back down until every last vote is counted. My father died in Vietnam so every vote can be counted. This is America; we must never surrender our democratic standards."

"What do you think?" Hussein Ibrahim asked Saleh Bowadi.

"They are making it too easy for us." Bowadi replied "These infidels are so incompetent. They have not changed no matter what they claim." The skinny 5'5" Bowadi weighed not even 150 pounds and was clean shaven. He shaved his mustache and beard before he and Ibrahim departed for the United States years earlier.

"Soon they will have something else to talk about. Maybe then they will realize that their idea of democracy is not such a good thing after all." Ibrahim noted. The 6'1" 180 pound man with jet back hair and tan skin was casually dressed just like Saleh in order to blend in with American society. The two men in fact did everything they could so they would not stand out like a sore thumb.

"They will be in for one rude awakening before the day is over with." Saleh said confidentially.

"That is an understatement my brother." Hussein observed. The two men were born in Saudi Arabia. They had been interested in joining al-Qaeda since they were ten year olds. After the September 11th attacks took place, their parents had filled their minds with anti-American beliefs for as long as they could remember. They had long been incensed by the American troops who long overstayed their welcome after Operation Desert Storm. All Hussein and Saleh could remember was the presence of the United States military. They had learned not only from their parents but from their textbooks that the United States was obsessed with world domination as well as oil in the Middle East. The two also learned that it was the United States desire to control all of the oil in the Middle East. This was reinforced by the 2003 invasion of Iraq by the United States as well as the continued presence of the American military long after Saddam Hussein was toppled. The two were taught that the Israeli Mossad and the CIA carried out the 9/11 attacks and not only framed al-Qaeda for the attacks, but used as an excuse to invade both Afghanistan as well as Iraq using it as a guise in order to control the oil in the Middle East. Hussein, Saleh, their families as well as Saudi Arabia feared that the War on Terror was also a war to eradicate Islam. This was also a feeling that was felt especially among the Wahhabi's. The Wahhabi's are followers of Wahhabism which is a puritanical sect of Islam. One that desires to teach Islam in the manner that it was revealed to the Prophet Mohammad in the early 600's AD. The Wahhabi revival became very evident during the siege of the Grand Mosque in Mecca back in November, 1979. The Wahhabi's claimed that the Mahdi who is the Islamic Messiah had come to usher in the last age of the world. The siege lasted for a couple of weeks until French troops who were enlisted by the government of Saudi Arabia and converted to Islam in order to even enter Mecca would storm the Grand Mosque and end the takeover. The takeover of the Grand Mosque had shaken Saudi Arabia to the core. The nation was divided and the Saudi Government infused Wahhabi Islam in every area of Saudi Arabian life in order to bridge the gap between the divisions which threatened to tear the nation apart.

Hussein Ibrahim and Salah Bowadi both grew up together and immigrated to Afghanistan and were trained by al-Qaeda. For years they learned the art of bomb making, surveillance, as well as being trained with machine guns and rocket launchers. The men had desired to someday carry out a 9/11 style attack but on a much larger scale. For the past few years since they were recruited for the Black Friday strike, they relocated to the United States and blended in with the rest of American Society while becoming law abiding citizens. There was never as much as a peep or a traffic ticket from the two. They made friends along the way while earning their trust among their circle of American friends. It was this mindset that made them among the least threatening among the American public. Their apartment was on the outskirts of Bethesda and had the look and décor of an apartment that would blend in with the other apartments in the area. The more recent furniture coupled with displays of seashores and the occasional Monet replicas were on the walls of their apartment. Also on the walls would be the occasional art house movie poster of a foreign movie which was mainly European or Latin American in nature. Other than that the apartment had the look of one where they could be able to move out with relative ease should they have to relocate elsewhere.

"I'm concerned that Cypress will be linked to this recount." Dick Tilden began as he was also watching CNN. He was aware that the voting machines that Cypress manufactured for the states whose votes were being disputed.

"Cypress is already linked to this recount." Dan Merkel replied as he then continued "I hope that another company also manufactured the voting machines that have been linked to this fiasco."

"I wish I could say that was the case." Tilden noted.

"You mean there isn't another company who manufactured the voting machines that have been linked to the disputed ballots in five states." Merkel wondered aloud.

"That would be correct." Tilden started as he then continued "Twenty states chose us to supply them with voting machines because of our integrity and now that is going to go by the wayside. No one will want to do business with us!" the founder and Chief Financial Officer of Cypress exploded "This is beyond intolerable! How is the internal investigation going?" he now demanded.

"We are looking into Gary Barton's role in this mess. We sent out someone to trail him in the months leading up to the recount." Dan Merkel replied.

"What did you find out?" Tilden inquired.

"I am going to learn more this afternoon." Merkel began "As soon I find out about Barton, you will be the first to know."

"Please do not even think to call me between eleven and four this afternoon." Tilden ordered "I will be testifying before that bi-partisan congressional committee that is investigating the disputed ballots."

"In that case, please call me once you are done with testifying before the committee." Merkel said as the conversation came to an end. Cypress, Incorporated was formed at the height of the dotcom boom during the late

1990's. Cypress was the shortened name for Cyber Express which provided internet service to those who resided in the southern United States. They gradually expanded to the southwestern United States as well as the Midwest and the Mid-Atlantic states. Cypress would fail in its repeated attempts to successfully tap into the Northeast especially New England, the Plains states as well as the Pacific Northwest and the West Coast. Despite these shortcomings, Cypress became a profitable niche company with its subscribers becoming not only the most loyal customers, but its most passionate ones at the same time. They began to branch out into the voting machines after the controversial 2000 presidential recount. Gradually Cypress began to market as well as sell voting machines while taking advantage of the recount as well as the need for new voting machines.

"I would like to sell 1,000,000 shares of Cypress and instead purchase 5,000,000 shares of Pan Arabian Oil." Ishmael Younis began as he placed the call from his office in Riyadh, Saudi Arabia to his broker in Zurich, Switzerland.

"I will take care of it right now." Hans Guibioso replied as he processed the transaction "I just found out that Cypress may have been involved in the voter tampering."

"Same here." Ishmael said as he continued "I think that Pan Arabian Oil would be the safer bet. It is undervalued as it is compared to the other oil stocks that are out there."

"Transaction done." Hans stated as he then asked "Is there anything else I can help you with Sheikh Younis?"

"Not at this time." Ishmael added as he then ended the call. The fifty eight year Saudi investment broker first took advantage of the securities game while attending King Khalid University in the mid-1980's. He quickly showed that he had a knack for making one successful investment after another as he first invested in Saudi-owned businesses. Soon after he branched out into Japanese-owned businesses. He then invested heavily in the dotcom boom during the late 1990's. Each time he had a knack for pulling out of his investments at the right time. Despite concentrating most of his investments in the Pacific Rim businesses as well as Indian and Chinese-owned corporations. Ishmael also became a prominent investor not only in Cypress, but also in the off shore companies that both were fronts for the heroin and Opium fields for Afghanistan and the drug cartels in Mexico, Columbia and Venezuela. Among his close friends in the Afghanistan drug trade included Khalid Isawi. Ishmael now turned on Al-Jazeera and watched it for a little while and then he switched to CNN and proceeded to watch it for most of the afternoon knowing that he had begun to set off another round of events. The first wave had already been completed. It was the second wave that would lead to the third wave and ultimately the fourth wave. The first wave took a while to complete and the final three would be completed within the next twenty four hours.

"Where do we stand?" Tim Lake asked Allan Bridges regarding the security at The Galleria. The two men were in

Bridges' office inside the security area of the Galleria Mall. Bridges only had papers on his grey metal desk which consisted of three drawers on the right side and a fourth in the middle of the desk. The office only had displays which promoted the mall as well as security requirements as prescribed by law. Bridges' office was deliberately devoid of pictures as well as any other effects that would identify him to those who ran amok of mall policy or allegedly ran amok of mall policy. This would not only protect Bridges from retaliation by any disgruntled individual or individuals who visited the office, but Bridges' family as well as his friends would be protected from any reprisals which may be carried out against Bridges and the other security personnel.

"We have our men prepared and every security apparatus in place." Bridges the heard of the Galleria security force responded. He had blond hair and blue eyes. He stood 6'0" and weighed 200 pounds.

"I am concerned about one thing." Lake began. The manager of the Galleria proceeded to continue on "There has been an increase in the presence of Arab looking individuals here in the past month. That presence has only increased in the past week." Lake was 6'5" and weighed 250 pounds. His wavy white hair and mustache helped give him an air of toughness while remaining fair as well as very open minded.

"What are you driving at." Bridges asked. His demeanor tended to be lackadaisical at best on occasion.

"How prepared are you should there be a Westgate Mall-style attack?" Lake inquired cautiously in reference to the September 2013 terrorist attack in Nairobi, Kenya by al-Shabab. The aforementioned terrorist group was an offshoot of al-Qaeda.

"As prepared as we can be." Bridges stated.

"That means you aren't prepared enough are you." Lake surmised.

"We have armed guards." Bridges said.

"How many?" Lake inquired as his patience was being tested.

"Ten to fifteen." Bridges responded.

"I'm afraid that that is not good enough. I must enlist the sheriff's department to have some more officers ready." Lake acknowledged. The Galleria Mall stood on a huge area of land which was previously a forest up until Colonial times. Through the years farms stood where the wooded area once dominated pre-colonial America. Then the farming industry suffered a gradual decline until the 1980's where the farms were abandoned since the families had either died off or went into another line of work. During the economic boom of the 1980's the land was bought by a developer who envisioned a shopping mall that would become the hub of business in the Southern Maryland-Northern Virginia-Washington, DC area. Once the Galleria Mall was construction and opened for business on October, 19 1987 it had suffered from a financial setback especially since the mall opened for business on the same day that the stock market crashed. It would take eight years and a change in ownership before the mall would begin to turn a profit. The new owners began a series of expansion projects in the late-1990's while capitalizing on the dotcom boom in the U.S. economy. During the recessions of the early as well as the late 2000's, the Galleria Mall continued to turn a consistent as well as an expanding profit annually while expanding and adding new stores that were not only cutting edge, but would be able to successfully cater to their clientele in the region. The Galleria's owners opened a series of malls in the Mid-Atlantic States that would consistently follow the business model that made the Galleria a phenomenal success. Although none of the malls were as successful as the Galleria, they would turn a consistent profit that increased annually. It was the owners of the Galleria that had the business savvy to be able to tap into the mindsets of the clientele in the regions that they opened their malls in and were able to make their respective malls a success at the same time. It was the Holiday shopping seasons that made the owners of the Galleria and other shopping malls in the region the most successful shopping mall developers in the United States.

Ohio Secretary of State Eric Watson was tossing and turning in his bed. He was nervous about the hearing that was to take place only hours from now. It was one that would set the tone for the possible expedient resolution to the allegations of voter fraud in Ohio. He was wondering how his counterparts in the other states were holding up this evening. Were they concerned that their states would also be found guilty of voter fraud? All these states whose GOP votes were being disputed all because of allegations of voter tampering.

This is a lot worse than the 2000 Presidential Recount. Would the Republican Party be forever known as the party that hijacks presidential elections in their favor when their candidate does not win fair and square?

"Honey, try to get some sleep." Donna Watson said to her husband.

"How can I know that I may be wrongly implicated in voter tampering?" Eric replied. Watson's brown hair, blue eyes and clean cut movie star good looks gave many an indication at first glance that he was in the wrong line of work. He usually wore dark suits which fit professionally well and had a tendency to wear a white dress shirt with a sequence of multi-colored ties which gave him a look of someone who seemed very happy in life.

"Look, I know that the votes were cast honestly. You know that they were cast honestly. God knows that they were cast honestly." Donna said as she drew on their Christian beliefs. Donna also had the look of an actress. Both Watson's were named sexiest political couple. She worked as a trustee for the Columbus City Council. She would be up for re-election within the next year. Her dark pantsuits and light color shirts were professionally appropriate. The couple had been married for almost twenty years despite being in their early forties. They were childless and too busy to even have children for that matter.

"Will the American people feel the same way? That is what I want to know." Eric added.

"Believe me, we are not a nation that resorts to voter tampering." Donna said confidentially.

"Tell that to Katherine Harris." Eric added in reference to the Florida Secretary of State back in 2000 "We haven't heard from her since." The Watson residence was in an affluent neighborhood in Columbus, Ohio. Their marble tables and post-Victorian chairs as well as the top of the line oak bookshelves and wooden floors along with the carpets that were brought in from the Orient made the house a throwback to the turn of the nineteenth to twentieth centuries. The book collection on the maple shelves has been a family heirloom which dates back to the early 1600's. Authors ranging from Plutarch, Plato and Aristotle right up to Tom Clancy, Robert Ludlum, John LeCarre, Vince Flynn, Brad Thor as well as Joel C. Rosenberg are placed in order of the date of publication throughout the eighteen shelf reading room in which a marble desk and a reclining chair dated back to the antebellum period.

12:30am

"Men." began Harvey Harrison "The chatter has died down." he noted in reference to Afghanistan "However there is still a cause for concern though. We are in the midst of a long and protracted recount. One that could very well divide this nation. It is obvious that al-Qaeda will somehow take advantage of this. We must be on our toes. I need your suggestions on how to beef up our security. We know that something may be in the works, but there is no credible threat out there as of this hour." Harrison was the 5'8", 175 pound leader of Ridgemont. He was clean shaven with gray hair as well as a ruddy appearance from his many years in the field tracking and capturing a considerable number of terrorists. Those present were in the twenty foot by twenty five foot conference room was the most start of the art room in Ridgeview. The twelve foot conference table was made of cedar and would seat up to ten people. The walls were covered with either state of the art computers as well as the newest tracking devices that have been made available to the intelligence community. The maximum of ten people were seated at the table. The group leader Harvey Harrison and the rest of his ten man crew including his assistant Reginald

Patterson occupied each seat at the table. The only topic of conversation in the room was what had been the sudden increase in chatter throughout the Middle East until the sudden silence which took place exactly nine hours earlier.

"As our intelligence has evolved so they have evolved." Ian Daley acknowledged "We need to beef up our security in the most vulnerable of places. I suggest that the malls would be a good start."

"You think so?" Graves said sarcastically "And where do we get the extra security from, your average Joe walking down the street."

"Enough!" Harrison said sternly.

"We need a more coherent plan." Daley urged.

"Would you like to come up here and run this meeting?" Harrison snarled.

"That would actually be a good place to start." Daley replied with contempt in his voice "I lost my wife on 9/11 and what is our intelligence community doing to prevent another attack." as there was silence in the room "Zilch." Ian noted "We need to improve our National Security and fast or there will be another attack like 9/11 but on a far more devastating scale."

"Has there been another attack since 9/11?" Harrison asked challenging Daley.

"Not yet, but if we are not careful, one will soon occur. We can't keep getting lucky like we've been since 9/11. The odds are against us." Daley exhorted.

"You do your job and I will do mine!" Harrison ordered "If there is anything you would like to say that would be a contribution for fighting this threat then say it. If not sit down and keep your mouth shut! Do I make myself perfectly clear!" he exploded.

"Just listen to what I have said about how to fight this war!" Daley noted.

"I am taking what you have said and put it on the record." Harrison noted as his tone became very irritated over the direction that the meeting was heading in. "Is there anyone else who feels the same way that I am not doing my job properly?" Everyone else in the room shook their head no in unison. "Alright then let us pick up where we left off." Harrison noted as the meeting went on for another twenty minutes. Harvey Harrison had long been a member of the National Security Department. He first joined the department during the early years of the Reagan Administration. Harrison slowly worked his way up the ladder. When Harrison first became a lower level manager of the National Security Department during the second year of the Clinton Administration, among his first hires was Art Graves as well as Ian Daley. Graves and Daley quickly became rivals of one another. Daley was more concerned about doing his job while Graves was more concerned about being a star employee while quickly moving up the ladder. This resulted in a lot of tension between the two men. At times the tension threatened to become counter-productive to the NSA. After 9/11, the Department of Homeland Security was created.

Harrison, Graves and Daley were transferred over to the new governmental agency. Daley was very gung ho in joining the Department of Homeland Security since his wife was killed while working in the Pentagon on 9/11. They were joined by a CIA agent who specialized in Counter-terrorism named Reginald Patterson. The four gradually moved up the ladder of the Department of Homeland Security. They were now among those who not only analyzed data but were very influential when it came to making recommendations about how to handle the latest terrorist threats while deciding where to allocate governmental resources to. They were now meeting once again to decide where they would allocate governmental resources in order to prevent another terrorist attack from taking place.

"Do you have any stories to share about Black Friday?" Irene Daley inquired.

"Believe me I have more than my share." the lady with the platinum blonde hair began "Before I continue my name is Harriet."

"I'm Irene." she responded "Nice to meet you."

"And I'm Irma." the younger twin by five minutes replied "It's nice to meet you too."

"Before I share my stories with you, do you have any questions about how to get through Black Friday? I see that you have the food and drink part well taken care of." Harriet noted.

"How crowded do the lines actually get?" Irene asked.

"Ten times more than what you see now by the time the first doors open." Harriet responded.

"Have there ever been any problems during the wait or when the doors first open?" Irma inquired.

"Other than the occasional rowdy person waiting in line and having too much to drink, nothing major during the wait. However, when it comes to the medical personnel arriving due to people getting hypothermia or passing out due to exhaustion or fatigue while waiting in line, I see at least ten for both cases every year." Harriet recalled.

"What time does it usually start?" Irene asked.

"I would say between one thirty and two o'clock in the morning." Harriet replied.

"That should begin in less than an hour from now." Irma mused aloud.

"You two should be fine. You're both well bundled up for the occasion. You have more than enough food. I would say don't be afraid to take frequent rest breaks. One of you rest up while the other waits in line. My daughter Sophie got a head start with the resting. I'm about to call her in a little while to switch places. You two might want to work out a similar plan." Harriet then suggested.

"We will definitely listen to your advice." Irene replied. Irene and Irma Daley were twenty six year old college students who had graduated from Johns Hopkins University and were now in the process of getting their doctorate's degree at Syracuse University only three months earlier. Since their mother's death, the twins had been withdrawn for the most part and had rarely socialized among their peers. However when they arrived in Syracuse, they befriended by another set of twins who had lost their mother in the World Trade Center on 9/11. Alexis and Andi Davies quickly befriended the Daley twins and quickly brought them out of their shell. Irene and Irma learned about how both Alexis and Andi lost their mother on 9/11 and saw how the two refused to let tragedy rule their lives. The Daley twins began to feel very enthusiastic about life once more. They became very outgoing and like the Davies twins became very popular among the SU graduate students not to mention among the undergraduates they befriended along the way. Alexis and Andi were now among the people who the Daley twins would do their Christmas shopping for on this very day.

House Speaker Nate Grumbly was reclining in the chair in his study while surfing the internet. Grumbly was fifty years old and had gray hair and brown eyes. His customary attire included silk suits which were professionally tailored as well as white silk shirts and dark silk ties. Grumbly was known by his nickname Silk. He was now scanning the NFL website looking over the scores. He was very pleased about Detroit losing to Denver 24-3, not happy about both Dallas beating New England 35-31 and his beloved Packers being blown out by the Bears 42-7 in the nightcap. The study had tan walls and a series of ten well organized bookshelves which ranged in subjects from ancient history and philosophy up to American History and Political Thought to Sports. The tan walls had white trim. The curtains were a dark brown given the fall and winter seasons. During the summers, the curtains would be white. There were displays of maritime scenes throughout the room which ranged from paintings to model ships. The maritime collection ranged from America and the West Indies to Europe, Africa and the Middle East. The works of the collection that also ranged from depictions of the Roman Era through the mid-1800's. Classical music was the only music that Grumbly would ever play while he was in the room. The combination of classical music and an old book brought the feeling of complete relaxation to him. It was in this very study that Nate Grumbly would be able to do his best thinking. Grumbly's cellphone. Grumbly then reached for his cellphone. He was about to place a call to his answering service in the nation's capital when the phone rang. Grumbly picked it up and then spoke to the person on the other line. The conversation would last for a few minutes. After it was over, Grumbly hung up the phone and placed a call to the answering machine in his office "I have decided to take a later flight back. I should be arriving around 4pm tomorrow. I have some matters to take care of tomorrow morning in Milwaukee. I apologize for any inconvenience that I may cause because of this." Grumbly then hung up the phone and proceeded to look at the website for another moment. He then retired for the evening. However, he received another call. Grumbly answered the call.

"Nate, it's me Kirk." Kirk Roberts began "The president would like to meet with you in the morning." Roberts was fifty eight years old and was tall and lanky. His light brown hair and blue eyes made him look youthful. His causal dress by Washington standards helped bolster the case that Roberts was youthful beyond his years.

"Tell the old windbag that I have a few things to take care of tomorrow morning first. After that I will take the noon flight back to DC." Grumbly replied.

"It's very important that you attend the meeting." Kirk noted.

"It was more important that President Wolcott chose Thomas as his running mate instead of remembering all that I did for him through the years." Nate shot back "I'm sorry, but I have more important matters to attend to."

"The meeting is about a grave national security matter." Roberts said.

"Look every time there has been a grave national security matter, nothing happened or it was a false alarm. Please don't bother me anymore for the night." Grumbly added as he hung up the phone. The tension between Nate Grumbly and Jeff Wolcott had lasted since the before the George H. W. Bush Administration when they worked on both the Mike Dukakis and the Al Gore campaigns respectively. They later parlayed their work in the 1988 presidential campaign into victories in the 1990 mid-term elections in both Wisconsin and Pennsylvania respectively. Both men were considered to be conniving and shrewd while becoming rising stars in the Democratic Party. Their political rivalry became even tenser during the 2008 presidential campaign when Wolcott worked on the Obama campaign while Grumbly worked on the

Hilary Clinton campaign. Four years ago, they were vying for the Democratic presidential campaign. The two were the last candidates standing and it resulted in a brokered convention. One that would last for three ballots until Wolcott barley had enough ballots for the nomination. Wolcott both courted the support of Texas Senator Vince Thomas whom they both offered the vice presidency too. Grumbly thought he had the perfect deal in place where Thomas would be able to convince enough delegates to support Grumbly until Wolcott blackmailed Thomas into endorsing him. Thomas not only threw his support as well as the delegates that he controlled to Wolcott, but this convinced Grumbly that the nomination process was rigged. Since then the only thing that consumed House Speaker Nathan Grumbly was revenge and the desire to bring down Jeffrey Wolcott once and for all.

"Men, we must begin final preparations to reclaim Taiwan." Sung Ju Luang began "I have come here directly from a meeting with the chairman of our military. He has informed us that Premier Ming has approved the excursion that is to take place within the next twenty four hours. As soon as he gives us the official order we will enter Taiwan and take it back." It was these words that made the soldier's day. Meanwhile in North Korea similar scenes were being played out among the various military branches. However it would not only involve South Korea, but Japan and the United States as well. At the same time, another teleconference was taking place throughout the Middle East. This time it would involve various Arab leaders discussing a covert military plot. As the meeting ended, they agreed to inform their military commanders to prepare their soldiers for war while awaiting their final orders to carry out the military strike.

2:00 am

"It's definitely getting colder." Irene began "Would you two like to join our team. We can increase the shifts by two since it is getting colder out here." The temperature was in the process of dropping a couple of degrees very rapidly.

"What do you think Sophie?" Harriet asked.

"I think that would be a great idea." Sophie replied as she was beginning to shiver.

"Sophie, you've got the first breather for the team." Irma stated.

"You got it. Thanks." Sophie responded as she then went to her Mom's tan van and began to drink the coffee that she had stashed in there.

"The merging of the teams usually happens around this time." Harriet observed aloud "By then some of the people in line becomes friends after talking for quite a while."

"Mom said that lifelong friendships are formed in times like these." Irene recalled.

"I couldn't agree with you more." Harriet laughed.

"Eric, you haven't slept a wink yet. Is this hearing distracting you?" Donna Watson inquired.

"The entire political landscape could change as a result of the hearing later this morning." Eric replied. "We cannot allow another four years of Wolcott in the White House. Unemployment has risen; the economy is not where it should be. The man has failed to keep his campaign promises. He has even upset the national security establishment by cutting back on funding for Homeland Security. There is going to be a monumental disaster is Wolcott is allowed to remain president for another term."

"I agree with you, this country needs Bob Freeman in the White House. I'm worried that this whole thing is taking quite a toll on you. You hardly finished your Thanksgiving dinner." Donna noted "Try to get some rest even if it means just shutting your eyes."

"I'll try honey." Eric said as he now closed his eyes and tried to remain still for the next few hours. For years Eric Watson had been a lower level politician who had worked for local as well as county politics. He had no desire to enter state or national politics for that matter until his older brother Ethan who he had always looked up to died of leukemia. Before Ethan Watson passed away, he recommended that his brother fill the post even on the caretaker level. The appointment was finalized six months ago. Eric Watson decided that he would only accept the post on condition that he would step down after the next gubernatorial election. The governor of Ohio accepted the terms of Eric's appointment. Since the recount and how Eric was doing his job, Eric was now being considered for a variety of higher level state positions and even has been mentioned as a congressional or even a senatorial candidate in the future. This further increased the pressure on the Ohio Secretary of State knowing that his life was enjoyable while serving on the local and county levels. Serving on the state level had made him very unhappy, but he knew that he was fulfilling the dying wish of his older brother.

"Agents Bishop and Downey, I need you to go to Langley and meet with Agents Townsend and Norman. There may be a terror threat looming." FBI Washington Bureau Chief Cliff Alfred began "You will help them look into the information form the threat matrix that they have received a little while ago." The meeting room in which the meeting was being conducted in had gray walls and a ten foot maple table. There were eight chairs in the soundproof room which was usually used for private conferences. It was for meetings like the one that Cliff Alfred was conducting with Agents Bishop and Downey that the room had been created for.

"Yes sir." they replied. The two agents then went into the underground garage at FBI Headquarters. "Your turn." Agent Bishop said to Agent Dawson."

"It was my turn the last time." Downey began "Tell me you didn't have too much to drink at dinner yesterday."

"I won't." Bishop grinned.

"I know that there's drama in your family, but . . ." Downey began as Bishop quickly cut him off "I did invite you over remember."

"I know how tense your family can be. I was backup last year. Never again." Downey noted as the two hopped into Downey's beige 2008 Honda Civic. They drove out of the parking lot and began the drive to Langley, Virginia. "I wonder what could be going on that we're being sent to Langley." he mused.

"I think something is about to go down." Bishop wondered aloud. He was 5'10" and weighed 170 pounds with brown hair and green eyes. He usually dressed casually when he was outside of work, but well-dressed professionally dressed while at work with the customary gray suit, white dress shirt and black tie.

"I think the malls could be attacked." Downey said. Downey was 5'9" and weighed 160 pounds. He also dressed casually when he was outside of work, but he wore dark suits with white dress shirts as well as dark ties.

"That is a possibility." Bishop began "I'm surprised that it hasn't been tried yet."

"We must never underestimate them." Downey recalled.

"That definitely goes without saying." Bishop noted as he then added "Do you think Director Francis will be replaced if Freeman becomes president?"

"I think Freeman will be much friendlier towards the intelligence community." Downey began "Wolcott's been cutting back gradually since he was inaugurated."

"I think Freeman would consider replacing Francis, but may back off once he realizes that there are worthy candidates out there." Bishop noted.

"I hope that you're right." Downey responded.

"I usually am." Bishop grinned. Agents Rob Bishop and Doug Downey quickly became friends when they were first recruited for the FBI. They were both raised under similar circumstances which were by single parent whom they were both very close to. Their love for Washington Nationals baseball, Washington Redskins football, Washington Wizards basketball and Washington Capitals hockey made them even closer. The two baseball, basketball, football and hockey fanatics quickly hit it off and requested that they would partner up together. For the past ten years they have been quite a formidable team for the agency. They would help crack many a case which involved terrorism. They were among a handful of agents that were not only able to work successfully with the CIA, but to co-exist and be friendly with them as well. It was this ability for the bridging of trust between the two rival agencies that helped the two successfully solve cases. This ability did not go unnoticed not only in the Department of Homeland Security, but also among the Department of National Intelligence who placed all of the intelligence and security agencies under one umbrella. Now they were going to help investigate what would become their biggest case to date and quite possibly in the history of national security.

"The crops have been very productive for us this year." Omar Dalwi began as he informed Khalid Isawi of the success of the heroin and opium plant in the farm that has been in the Isawi family since the 1600's. The farm was the oldest in

Afghanistan. It also served as the main farm for Khalid's chain of heroin and opium farms. They were strategically placed throughout Afghanistan and were managed by a different person who was ordered to plant vegetables at each farm and sell it at the marketplaces throughout the country in order to make it look like a legitimate business. The produce business also became a widely successful one for Isawi in which enormous sums of money were made in the process. At the same time, many Afghanistan citizens were unaware that their money not only went to radical Islamic causes, but also to the drug trade in Afghanistan, Columbia, Mexico and Venezuela as well as supporting terrorist operations run by al-Qaeda and investments in American corporations such as Cypress with the intention of bringing about the fall of the United States of America in the process.

3:00am

"Here we go!" Irene Daley said to Irma as the two were about to make their mad dash into target.

"Before you go in, remember don't be like everyone else rushing in. If you rush in, you will likely either get hurt or risk hurting someone else. Then your strategy for buying will be guaranteed to be ruined." Harriet said as she dispensed one more piece of advice to the twins. As almost everyone rushed in, Irene, Irma, Harriet and Sophie calmly walked in as though they were in a state of complete oblivion as to what was occurring around them. As laptops as well as notebook laptops were being quickly scarfed up, the Daley twins took their shopping carts and began to pick off items on their shopping list one by one. With each passing second, they were quickly crossing off the majority of their Christmas shopping lists that the two had spent weeks preparing. Just then they saw one laptop left. "I know who would like this." Irene said as she picked it up and then placed it her cart "Merry Christmas Irma."

"How did you know that I needed a new laptop?" Irma gasped.

"Trust me; you've had that other one for like six years." Irene remarked.

"It's brought a lot of good luck to me through the years." Irma noted.

"But it's on its last legs." Irene stated "You can thank me later." With that the twins continued on with their shopping.

"Ian." Reggie Patterson began "Harrison would like to see you in his office at once." Daley then left his station and made his way to Harvey Harrison's office. "What is your take on everything?" Patterson then inquired.

"They are definitely up to something." Ian replied "I don't exactly what, but al-Qaeda is playing it very close to the vest. They are not tipping their hand to anyone. If I were a betting man, I would say that the malls are going to be hit today given the increased and then sudden decrease in chatter."

"I think this should be brought up to Harrison." Patterson stated as the two now entered Harrison's office. Harvey Harrison's office consisted of off white walls with dark green curtains. The Birch desk, as well as the walls and bookshelves were plastered with a combination of pictures, mementos as well as the various awards that he received throughout his career. Even numerous citations were framed as well as displayed throughout the office.

"Ian, I know you have been around longer than most people here. I know that I can trust you to give a good analysis about what could happen." Harrison started as he then paused and took a deep breath. "What is your take on everything?"

"I think we could be dealing with a two pronged attack at the very least. That is usually the M.O. of al-Qaeda." Daley began as he then added "I wouldn't be surprised if the malls are attacked."

"I don't think they have enough people to attack all of the malls." Harrison responded with a twinge of sarcasm in his voice.

"It would be a good way to pull law enforcement away for al-Qaeda to complete their deadly one-two punch." Daley noted.

"I don't think they have enough operatives to pull it off." Harvey scoffed.

"Sir, they have been recruiting Americans for years. If you have enough disgruntled citizens who are fed up with the government . . ." Daley started as Patterson cut him off "I think what Daley is trying to say is that the operatives may assume that they are working for the militias when in fact they are working for al-Qaeda."

"I see." Harrison mused aloud "They cannot be that clever."

"They were clever enough to bring box cutters on board and use our planes as guided missiles on 9/11!" Daley shot back "I am sure that they are clever enough to recruit Americans as believing that they are members of a militia not al-Qaeda. They have recruited African-Americans for their cause knowing that . . ."

"I will carry the ball from here!" Patterson retorted "I know that al-Qaeda has infiltrated the African-American community and recruited members for their cause. They are preying on the disenfranchisement of my race in order to increase their membership dramatically."

"I think that these scenarios are far-fetched that they are better left to authors such as Tom Clancy." Harrison snarled.

"But Tom Clancy wrote of a hijacked plane crashing into the U. S. Capital building in his novel *Debt of Honor*. That was published seven years before the 9/11 attacks took place. Yes, authors write scenarios that the terrorists ultimately pick up on and carry out down the road. Why don't we start preparing for those scenarios immediately after they are published to begin with? This would save us lives in the future not to mention untold millions, even billions of dollars in damages after the attacks take place. Why does it always take a catastrophic failure before we even begin to take action? Why don't we take preventative measures to ensure that these things do not take place? We've had happen before. It will happen again and again if we do not learn from the mistakes from the past!" Daley argued.

"Who appointed you to chair the Department of Homeland Security?" Harrison snarled.

"I was only bringing up some valid points." Daley protested.

"You've brought up more than enough for one lifetime. This conversation is over." Harvey said dismissing Daley and Patterson. Daley then left and Patterson quickly followed him "You had to play the race card didn't you?"

"I was only bringing up a valid fact!" Daley stated defending himself "Besides you made a brilliant argument as well, if I am not mistaken."

"I was only trying to cover for you!" Patterson stated "I don't know how and where you come up with some of your ideas, but this is beginning to wear thin with everyone here. How do we even begin to utilize the resources for your far-fetched scenarios?"

"September 11th was considered a far-fetched scenario but look what happened." Daley shot back "No one thought that hijacked planes would ever be used as missiles for crying out loud."

"Take a break Daley. Better yet, take the day off." Patterson ordered.

"Someday you will appreciate my efforts. Trust me." Daley said with contempt in his voice. Ian Daley had been long consumed with preventing another terrorist attack from taking place. This would date back to that fateful September day back in 2001 when his wife Eileen was killed while working in the Pentagon. Once George W. Bush announced the creation of the Department of Homeland Security, Ian begged his superiors to be transferred to Homeland Security in order to avenge the death of his beloved Eileen while preventing another terrorist attack from taking place. Since then Ian feel at peace knowing that he was fighting the War on Terror while making a contribution to it. For years he felt that he had the most rewarding job in the world. Now he was absolutely convinced that this feeling that he previously had was nothing more than a mirage. Daley felt very duped that the agency who he worked for betrayed not only him, but the American people at the same time. Ian was now feeling disillusioned not only his work, but his life at the same time. Ian no longer knew who he could trust. This was among the lowest feeling that one could feel. The feeling that all has worked for was for nothing. There was one person who Ian still trusted. He would now wait an hour before he would call Tim Lake who he had known since the two were college students.

"I see that our pals from the FBI have come up here to help us." Agent Townsend said to Agent Norman as they saw Agents Bishop and Downey from the FBI outside the meeting room on the ground floor at Langley.

"At least we can trust them." Agent Norman noted as Agents Bishop and Downey entered the room "We are so glad to see you." Norman said as both he and Agent Townsend felt a sense of relief over the arrival of their counterparts from the Federal Bureau of Investigation.

"We heard the Langley's been having some trouble deciphering the latest terror threat so we were sent here to help our good friends." Agent Bishop replied.

"There was a spike in chatter throughout the region especially in Afghanistan." Agent Townsend began "Suddenly around three pm yesterday afternoon our time of course it went completely silent. We have been here ever since for the past twelve hours now trying to figure this whole thing out."

"Could you fill us in about any words that you may have picked up along the way?" Agent Downey then asked.

"That is where we are having the most problems. They seem to be discussing about a death of a key operative due to natural causes along the lines of old age. We became greatly concerned once the chatter went completely silent." Agent Norman added.

"I think we can rule out a funeral at this stage of the game. I don't think that they would bury their dead on their holy day of the week." Agent Bishop said.

"I think we can also rule out a funeral lasting this long." Agent Townsend acknowledged.

"We have no idea about what they intend to do and when they intend to carry it out not to mention where they will carry it out for that matter." Agent Norman stated as a he chimed in on the discussion.

"Whatever could happen I think it is going be much more monumental than 9/11 and they are deliberately speaking cryptically in order not to be detected." Agent Downey added "By the way did you get the name of the operative who supposedly passed away?"

"We looked up the name of Farouk al-Mokqui and there are five known persons who share his name. None of them seem to be on any of our watch lists nor are they known members of al-Qaeda. We have questioned all five Farouk al-Mokqui's and it is safe to say that they are clean." Agent Townsend stated.

"If so, then what are they up to?" Agent Bishop mused aloud "That is what everyone wants to know and now."

"The only concern is that the malls may be attacked and we don't even have any proof whatsoever that the malls are even an intended target today, this weekend or even during the Christmas season for that matter." Agent Norman began "Need I remind you of the terrorist attack on the Westgate Mall in Kenya back in Fall 2013." he recalled. With that the conversation continued on for the next ten minutes.

"I thought what you just preached was very timely." Ishmael Younis said to the Sunni cleric Abdullah.

"Thank you." the cleric replied as he then added "Thank you for you very generous contribution. I see that business is still going very well for you."

"You are welcome as always." Younis responded.

"How is the operation coming along?" the cleric then inquired.

"It is about to be brought into fruition with phases two, three as well as four about to take place within the next few hours."

"This is such wonderful news to hear." Abdullah began as he added "May Allah bless you and our brothers throughout the world for the operation that they about to complete for Allah. The imam then departed from Younis. Younis in turn returned to his office where he would remain glued to his television set until the operation was declared a success.

6:00am

"Good morning and welcome to Fox and Friends." the FOX news anchor began "Today is the day that the Ohio State Supreme Court will hear arguments regarding the disputed ballots for six counties. At ten am, arguments will begin for whether the disputed ballots should be counted or not."

Meanwhile Tim Lake was watching the live coverage on FOX News. His office was near the food court of the Galleria. Lake's office consisted of pictures of family and friends as well as mementos from the Baltimore Orioles and Ravens sports teams. The papers that were on his desk were neatly organized. The walls were light blue and the trim was navy blue. The bookshelves were made of cedar and had books ranging from business management to self-improvement. The only window in his office would overlook the lobby which in turn overlooked the food court. Lake began to think about how he first joined the company as a member of the security force of the Samson Property Group as a security guard. He knew that there would hardly be any corruption working for a private security firm. Lake felt very much at peace knowing that he did not have to deal with corruption in the police force anymore. His partner was a very corrupt police officer who almost brought Tim Lake down years earlier. Since Lake felt very betrayed that he was set up that he almost left law enforcement all together until an uncle of his convinced him to joint SPG. Since then Lake moved up the chain of command due to his hard work as well as his strong sense of ethics at the same time. Once the opening for the director of mall security opened up at the Galleria Mall, Lake was recommended for it. He would soon be offered the job which he accepted without hesitation. Within five years, Lake was promoted to Manager of the Galleria Mall. Despite the stress of the holiday season every year, this was the happiest that Tim Lake has ever been. However with the conversation that transpired with Allan Bridges a few hours earlier, Lake was now concerned that all of his hard work would soon come undone. He decided to call his old friend Ian Daley. Daley quickly picked up the phone and said "Tim, I was about to call you. I need to talk to you about something.

"Actually we can both help each other out this morning." Lake began as he then paused "Ian, I need your advice about something." Tim Lake began.

"How can I help you?" Daley inquired as he was watching Fox and Friends.

"How would you combat a potential terror threat as the manager of a mall if the director of security has failed to prepare for such a scenario?" Lake asked.

"First of all, I would order the director to be more aggressive in this kind of situation. However, it's Black Friday and bringing in a new director of security and retraining the staff would be quite a challenge. Anyways, I would start looking for a new director." Daley replied.

"How is the job at Homeland Security?" Lake asked.

"Not good at all. I tried to warn them that the malls may be attacked today and they did not take me seriously." Daley noted.

"The job for Director of Security is yours if you want it." Lake offered.

"I will accept the offer should the Department of Homeland Security elects to fire me. I think is what they're going to do." Daley mused aloud.

"You've put in a lot of time there." Lake observed "I think that you can do better and deserve better than what you have received."

"Meanwhile, the State Supreme Courts in Florida, Pennsylvania, Arizona and West Virginia will meet over the weekend in an emergency session to hear arguments regarding the disputed ballots in their respective states." the FOX News anchor added "Today is Black Friday the busiest shopping day of the year. Tens of millions of Americans will be converging on the nation's malls in hopes of getting that special gift for a bargain.

"This day is usually our most stressful one." Lake added as he was watching Fox and Friends.

"I take it you're watching FOX News as well." Daley noted as he heard the sound of the TV in the background on the other end of the cellphone line."

"Yes." Lake replied "I have it on in my office. I'm just finishing up some paperwork." Lake said "I will call you if I need some more advice." he replied as he hung up the phone.

"Those infidels will definitely be receiving a special gift alright. It will have to be just more than a month earlier than planned." Hussein Ibrahim began as he and Saleh Bowadi were both watching Fox and Friends as well.

"Today is definitely going to give Black Friday a whole new meaning." Bowadi replied as the two men were making last minute preparations for their mission.

"Were you able to sleep?" Ibrahim asked Bowadi.

"I woke up a few times." Saleh replied "Were you able to sleep as well my brother?"

"I woke up a few times myself." Hussein responded "Are you nervous about today?"

"I'm a little bit nervous." Bowadi stated "Are you?"

"Yes, I'm slightly nervous." Ibrahim began "It will be over in a few hours though. It's just waiting for the go ahead that is nerve wracking."

"I couldn't agree with you more." Saleh added as the two continued to watch FOX News while awaiting their signal.

"Honey, were you able to sleep?" Donna Watson asked Eric was he began to get out of bed.

"If I got a few minutes then I was very lucky." Eric replied as he added "I don't want to be there today. All I want to do is actually get some sleep."

"Have you thought about resigning?" Donna inquired.

"If it were only that easy." Eric wished "But . . ."

"But what?" Donna mused.

"I can't resign in the middle of this crisis." Eric started "Believe me that thought has crossed my mind though."

"How about after this whole thing is done?" Donna suggested.

"I did promise that I would serve out for the remainder of Ethan's first term." Eric noted.

"How about taking a leave of absence?" Donna thought aloud.

"You know what." Eric said "I'm going to do just that. Thank you!" he said as he began to start the day.

Ayman al-Zawahiri walked outside the concrete slab building which needed a new paint job. The building overlooked one of the many mountainous regions inside Afghanistan. It was this particular mountainous region that was near the Pakistani border. The building was in a larger village which was crowded with people. He walked around outside the building, but within the fenced area where he would escape detection on this late Friday afternoon while anticipating the moment when the death of his comrade

Osama bin Laden would finally be avenged. Meanwhile he saw one of his couriers from a distance. The young boy was now walking up to al-Zawahiri briskly. Al-Zawahiri began to slow down until the courier was right in front of him.

"Sir." the young boy began.

"How can I help you child?" al-Zawahiri asked.

"I have a note for you." the young boy replied as he handed it to the leader of al-Qaeda. Ayman al-Zawahiri opened the note and then put it in his satchel and said "Thank you." while handing him a few dinars.

"Thank you!" the young boy gushed knowing that his family would have enough money to eat for a few months. With that he began the long trek home. Ayman al-Zawahiri then walked back into the compound and said "The signal will be delivered soon." to one of his comrades. Now we wait to see if the mission is a success." Now al-Zawahiri took out his Koran and began to read it in order to remain relaxed given how the events of the next few hours could play out.

"This is very frustrating." Agent Bishop began as he and Agent Downey both reviewed the chatter that Langley received until it suddenly went quiet. "We cannot seem to figure out what they intend to do as well as where and how."

"Imagine how we feel." Agent Townsend replied "We have went through every possible code and not to mention bringing in the best code breakers to figure out this whole thing and so far we have come up with nothing."

"Obviously al-Qaeda has become much smarter than we are. They have once again proven that they had the ability to evolve and become a more formidable enemy. Did you have any agents or informants in place inside any of the al-Qaeda camps?" Agent Downey inquired.

"We have a few but none of them are in the know of anything that may be in the works. They have been on the peripheral for years though. At least two of them are on the brink of being brought in closer to al-Qaeda though." Agent Norman added.

"Of all the times for this to happen. As always we are two seconds too late." Agent Downey said in frustration.

"I'm afraid that it is becoming a way of life for us." Agent Townsend acknowledged "We are so sick and tired of it as it is."

"Look at how crowded it is!" Irene Daley began in reference to the parking spaces at the Galleria Mall "And it is shortly after seven o'clock in the morning."

"Imagine what it is going to be like in a few hours." Irma noted as Irene knew that she would have to park back further in one of the parking lots than planned.

"At least we're here now. That's all that matters. We can find a parking space with relative ease." Irene started "If we were to arrive here in an hour from now . . ."

"I don't even want to think of it right now." Irma stated as Irene began to pull into a parking space. The twins then got out of the car and began to walk into what was quickly becoming a very crowded mall as a parade of cars were beginning to arrive at the mall. Irene and Irma now entered the mall and saw a Salvation Army volunteer ringing his bell as though he was signaling for donations. Both Irene and Irma each put two dollars in the kettle.

"Thank you." the middle aged African-American male smiled.

"You're welcome." both Daley twins replied as they entered the Galleria Mall through the main entrance. The two were now enamored with the Holiday displays throughout the mall. Each store as well as each kiosk was elaborately decorated. Holiday decorations were prominently displayed in the hallways of the mall. It was the center court display which left both Irene and Irma spellbound. The Christmas Village display consisted of a wooden red gate which surrounded the village. Artificial snow covered every inch of the village while it was less than an inch deep. Miniature gingerbread houses were mixed in along with miniature Victorian-era homes which evoked memories of Charles Dickens' *A Christmas Carol* while candy canes and model miniature elves and Victorian-era statues of 1800's Christmas carolers were spread out through the miniature village. The Christmas carolers had microphones connected to a sound system. At the center of the village an elevated platform with a stairway on both sides held a life sized Nativity scene with Mary, Joseph, the Christ child, an Angel at the center of the stable against the wall with the manger in front of the angel. The Three Wise Men were off to the left side of the manger with the Shepherds and their sheep off to the right side. The donkey and horse reclined outside the stable with three camels standing by the Wise Men. Below the Nativity was a large red and green chair where Santa Claus would sit and greet multitudes of children who shared their Christmas gift list with kindly old St. Nicholas who was flanked by a helper on each side of his chair. This very display was the main attraction not only for the Galleria Mall during the Holiday season, but throughout Maryland.

"Wow!" Irene gasped while she and Irma were checking out the display "I have never seen anything so beautiful."

"I know!" Irma gushed "I feel like this is a dream and yet it is so awesome to see Christmas Village." as the Daley twins began to walk throughout the village while taking pictures.

"This captures every essence of Christmas." Irene said.

"I wish we had appreciated this much earlier." Irma noted.

"We did appreciate this much earlier. Mom always took us there. We could never set foot in here since she was killed until now." Irene recalled. The two twins were now wandering throughout the village as though they were little girls wandering throughout a toy store. Some of the people who were walking Christmas Village were observing the Daley twins wandering through the village. One mother now turned to her two children and said "Remember no matter how old you are, have the enthusiasm for Christmas that these two women are having right now."

"Yes Mommy." the seven year old boy and his five year old sister replied in unison. "Can we play in there?"

"Yes." she replied as they entered the village and began a parade of shoppers who quickly entered Christmas Village.

Dan Merkel hardly slept this very evening. The shock over the realization that Cypress may have deliberately tampered with the votes in Florida, Virginia, Pennsylvania, Ohio and Arizona was so much for him to bear that it virtually left him numb. All he kept thinking about was how his investigators could have failed not only to figure out that Gary Barton was up to no good, but that they failed to stop him in the process. As he now got out of his bed and walked shiftlessly downstairs to the living room, he kept thinking about how he was going to be fired from Cypress as well as has to look for another line of work. But who would hire him knowing the role that he unwittingly played in the voter fraud that had taken place only seventeen days earlier. Daniel Patrick Merkel was only fifty years old, but had always prided himself in conducting himself ethically in everything that he has done in life. Merkel had attended Harvard and was first in his class. He had been a mid-level manager for International Business Management which was better known by its acronym IBM until he was laid off. He was then hired by the Eastman Kodak Company and lasted there until the massive layoffs of the 2000's. Cypress quickly hired Dan Merkel and he has been employed by the company ever since. Merkel quickly shot up the corporate ladder and became Chief Financial Officer only three years ago. The stress that was brought on with the allegations of voter tampering began when a protégé of Dan Merkel, Bruce Callahan came to him and informed him of the suspicious conduct of Callahan's own protégé Gary Barton only two and a half months earlier. All Merkel kept thinking about was the conversation that occurred during the weekly lunches that Merkel and Callahan would have at O'Toole's restaurant.

"So how is everything in your department running?" Merkel asked Callahan.

"It's running smoothly for the most part. Sales are increasing for the CyRePress eReader that was released last month. There have been very few glitches in the program. The techies have quickly taken care of each one though. The only criticism that we have received is that we should have come out with it years ago." Callahan replied.

"If that is the only criticism that we have received about the CyRePress then we are doing something right." Merkel noted as he then asked "How is Donald feeling?" he asked in reference to Donald Rodgers' radiation for stomach cancer.

"I just visited him yesterday. He is coming along well. Only three more sessions to go before he is done." Callahan responded.

"When is his next session going to take place?" Merkel wondered aloud.

"Friday." Callahan noted.

"In that case I will be visiting Donald tomorrow afternoon. I will make a point of doing so." Merkel said as he then changed the subject by asking "How is your protégé Gary Barton doing?"

"That is what I wanted to talk to you about." Callahan said.

"Is everything alright with our friend?" Merkel inquired.

"I'm afraid that everything is far from alright." Callahan stated.

"How so?" Merkel then asked.

"Callahan's work has been slipping dramatically. He seems to have been making some serious lapses in the past month. If I didn't know any better I would say that he is still angry about being passed over for that promotion and is out to sabotage the company because of it." Callahan acknowledged as he was feeling very concerned over his protégé.

"He wasn't qualified for the promotion Levin was." Merkel noted "The only thing that prevented Barton from being promoted was his lack of managerial experience."

"Just don't tell him that whatever you do, he will completely lose it." Callahan began "When Barton was told that he was passed over the promotion he flew into an uncontrollable rage. Since then it has been all downhill from there. How do I go about handling this? I am at my wits end with Barton as it is. I don't know what to do anymore."

"I know an excellent private investigator. I will call him and have him give you a call."

"Thank you." Callahan replied as they continued on with their weekly lunch.

"What did you find out about Barton?" Dan Merkel asked Bruce Callahan a month later as they were having another of their Wednesday weekly lunches at O'Toole's.

"It seems that Gary Barton now has some new associates." Bruce began "A few of them are lobbyists who are known to be

unsavory at best. They are well connected to Governor Freeman as well as President Wolcott."

"So Gary is playing both sides of the political fence." Merkel mused aloud "What else have you found about our friend?"

"It seems that he has been associating with a person on the nation's terrorist watch list." Callahan continued.

"What?" Merkel snapped.

"I am afraid that Gary Barton has been having frequent contact with a person who has recently been put on the nation's terrorist watch list." Callahan said repeating what he had previously said.

"Well I hope the feds are watching Barton because of this!" Merkel exploded.

"There is not much they can do right now, but they are now watching Barton's movements very closely." Callahan acknowledged "I spoke to human resources and they cannot terminate him because of the lawsuit that would be brought upon us as a result of doing so."

"Well our hands are definitely tied because of this." Merkel snarled "We need to explore some gray area of the law and take action from that front instead." He suggested "And fast. I will speak to the owner as well as our legal department and we will proceed from there."

"Well how did you meeting with the owner and the legal department go?" Bruce Callahan asked Pat Merkel.

"I am afraid that their hands are tied about this as well. They cannot do a thing unless there is no question that there is suspicious

activity taking place. They don't want to be sued." Merkel replied as he felt very grim.

"That is a limp excuse!" Callahan snapped "What are they waiting for? A terrorist attack to take place for crying out loud. They will definitely be sued by then and lose a lot more from the victim's families then they would have lost from Gary if they had let him go! Is this some flipping joke to them!"

"They are doing this ethically. I am not the biggest fan of how they are going about this." Merkel conceded "I know that I have always been an ethical person, but with these developments I am beginning to think twice about it."

"You are not the only one who feels that way right about now." Callahan stated "If there was only something we could do without crossing the ethical boundaries."

"I am definitely with you there." Merkel acknowledged "And I am constantly trying to come up with an idea about how to handle Barton."

"I am doing the same thing as well. His performance hasn't dropped so badly nor has it lasted long enough to let him go." Callahan began "We must come up with something and fast."

"We are definitely on the clock right now when it comes to doing something about Barton." Merkel noted as the two continued on with their weekly lunch.

Merkel now turned on the television to Music Choice and channeled surfed to the Holiday Music Channel and began to listen to Christmas music in an attempt to keep his mind off what was going on.

"Dick, this is going to get very nasty." Irving Rosenbaum began as Tilden's attorney then continued "They have spent a week and a half digging up dirt on Cypress as well as its employees. I have no question that the best way to handle this would be to be honest with what you know and don't be afraid to mention Gary Barton along the way and the legal department as well as human resources kept you hamstrung on what to do. I know that there will be questions even after your complete your testimony to the congressional committee but as long as you are completely honest with them you will have nothing to lose especially in the long run." The two were standing in line at the Jet Blue terminal at Miami International Airport for the flight from Miami to Washington, DC that would depart at 7:15.

"What could happen in the short term?" Tilden inquired.

"You could possibly be indicted for voter fraud and face trial. However, you could also convince enough people that you are actually telling the truth and they will believe the truth." Rosenberg stated "The bottom line is that it could go either way today. That is why I urge you to be truthful about what you knew about Gary Barton as well as the voting scandal. You must also be firm as well as emphatic while answering every question. Do not let them get you rattled. That is what they are going to try to do. The goal of that committee is to throw you off to the extent that your story will not be credible and that the already growing wrath of the American people against Cypress will grow dramatically." Rosenberg explained as he then briefly paused and then added

"I will be by your side the entire time. Listen to me and do as I say and everything will be alright."

"Yes." Tilden replied as the line at the Jet Blue terminal was quickly moving. There would only be eight people who would board the flight to the nation's capital. All but two of them would be lobbyists.

"There will be a taxi waiting for us as soon as we arrive at Reagan International Airport. It will take us directly to the Capital Building. Once we arrive, we will go through a series of screening procedures where we will be checked for weapons. After that we will be escorted to a holding room where we will wait until we are called to testify in front of the congressional committee. After we complete our testimony, we will then leave for a restaurant inside DC and have lunch. Then we will board a flight back to Miami and once we arrive we can return to our families." Rosenberg stated as he explained to Tilden the itinerary for the day.

"What time do you think we will be home with our families?" Tilden asked.

"I would say be ten this evening." Rosenberg said as the two showed their boarding passes. Irving Rosenberg and Dick Tilden then boarded their flight and sat down in the coach section where they would now wait for their flight to take off.

8:00am

"Mr. President." Pat Ryan began as the Director for Homeland Security continued on saying "The chatter that we have been listening to in the past few weeks in Afghanistan has suddenly stopped. There is a strong indication that al-Qaeda is on the brink of carrying out an attack, but no one has any idea where it will take place." Ryan always wore black suits, white shirts as well as either a red, blue or gray tie. He was 6'4" and weighed 235 pounds. His salt and pepper hair and wire rimmed glasses made him look like a governmental official. The Oval Office had an American flag to the right of President Wolcott. Facing the president were white bookshelves which were full of books ranging from every subject matter possible. The bookshelves blended in with the white walls. The walls had red trim and meshed in nicely with a blue floor which had the presidential seal on the middle of the floor which was in the middle of the Oval Office. There was a doorway on the left side of the president's desk. It would lead not only to a bathroom, but also to the Lincoln Bedroom which was on the other side of the bathroom. President Wolcott had spent many an evening leaving the Lincoln Bedroom in the middle of the night in order to work at his desk which was only a very short walk away. On this very morning President Wolcott was still in a very sour mood over the fact that his Thanksgiving dinner with his family was interrupted the newest terror threat by al-Qaeda. What made this latest threat even more maddening was the fact that no one exactly what the threat would entail not to mention no one knew where it would occur.

"I think the word that you're looking for is places." President Wolcott began "al-Qaeda has a history of carrying out attack in two different places at once." Wolcott had gray hair, blue eyes and wore a black suit usually with a sky blue or a silver tie. He was 6'0" and weighed 190 pounds.

"Although they have shifted their strategy in recent years, we must never let down our guard. No one has been able to pick up on any words that may signal where the attacks will take place not to mention how they will attack us."

"Do you have any code breakers working on it?" Wolcott then inquired.

"We have our best code breakers but they have had no luck cracking the code." Ryan added.

"You mean to tell me that you have your best people working on this and you have failed to yield any results as of yet?" the president blurted.

"I'm afraid so." Ryan noted "It's difficult to properly run my department when you cut funding for it considerably."

"May I remind you that I am trying to have it run more efficiently." Wolcott stated with an edge of anger in his voice "How dare you question my authority."

"I should say how dare you limit funding for my department. This alone has increased the risk of a terrorist attack being carried out!" Ryan shot back.

"This meeting is over." President Wolcott began "Dismissed!"

"Remember it's your fault if the United States is attacked once again." Ryan added as he stormed out of the office. He then breezed his way out of the White House and briskly walked to his car. He drove out of the White House and then placed a call to the Director of National Intelligence Chet Jackson.

"How did the meeting with the president go Pat?" Jackson inquired. He was 5'11" and weighed 215 pounds. His red hair and green eyes gave him the look of someone who had just emigrated from Ireland. He usually wore a light gray or brown suit as well as a crisp white dress shirt and ties which would match the suit that he would wear on a given day.

"It was a complete disaster." Ryan replied "The man is questioning the ability of my department when it comes to pinpointing a specific terrorist threat."

"It's impossible to pinpoint where a potential attack will take place when they are not dropping any hints as to where it will occur." Jackson noted "Keep plugging away. You will find out one way or another."

"I will." Ryan stated.

The most recent presidential campaign had been the tensest one. In fact it was still going on. The Republican primaries had marked the second time in as many presidential election cycles that the race for the nomination was so close that it would take a brokered convention to decide it. In fact Virginia Governor Bob Freeman won on the fourth ballot after the other two candidates realized that they would not be able to secure enough delegates for the nomination. One had no shot at all, but chose to continue on campaigning in order for his health insurance initiative would be on the GOP platform. The other candidate felt that he was the alternative to Freeman. The candidate who held out due to his heath care proposal began to see his support evaporate to the other two candidates while his proposal was accepted for the GOP platform. He bowed out knowing that he had achieved his goal. The regional candidates and favorite sons took up enough votes that the last remaining candidate would not be able to secure the nomination. After a few hours of negotiations, he dropped out in favor of the vice presidential nod. This unified the Republican Party going forward. The Freeman-Lafferty ticket quickly became a very formidable one. It resulted in the Wolcott-Thomas ticket becoming vulnerable. The election would be so close that the debates resulted only in fickle support for the candidates which would quickly change each day. On Election Day, not only were five states too close to call, but neither candidate received a mandate from the popular vote. The third party candidates ensured that this neither main party candidate would receive fifty percent of the vote.

The Galleria Mall was crowded as though it was a normal Saturday afternoon. Irene and Irma Daley were now entering Macy's and were checking out the clothing department for gifts for both Alexis and Andi.

"We really need to get our friends something very special." Irene began as she and Irma were acknowledging the impact they had on their lives.

"I know that they need sweaters." Irma noted as the two made their way to the Women's department in order to find two special sweaters for their special friends. They were now checking the discount's for the sweaters. I think those are too conservative." She noted for the first set of sweaters.

"How about these?" Irene suggested as she motioned Irma over.

"They definitely look very colorful!" Irma noted.

"Now we have to look for a petite for both." Irene said as they quickly found two identical light multi-color sweaters "I know they will love these."

"Wait what about these two?" Irma then mentioned.

"Let me see!" Irene beamed as she checked the other two sets of petite sweaters "I think we should buy them both!"

"I agree there!" Irma said as they agreed to buy both sets of sweaters for both sets of twins.

"What do you have to report?' the chief of the CIA Bureau in Washington, DC inquired of Agents Bishop and Downey.

"We are as perplexed as they are." Agent Bishop replied.

"How so?" the Chief then asked.

"However they are doing this, they are issued their codes in such a way that it is beyond decipherable." Bishop continued "Even the best code breakers are having trouble deciphering them. They have brought in their best technical wizard in order to crack the code. So far that isn't working as well. We are up against one very formidable enemy this time."

"We have already sent in our best people for this." the Chief began "We have not made any headway though. If your people have any suggestions, please let us know immediately so we can prevent this threat of threats from being carried out." The Chief was a Native American who was 5'10" and was skinny like a reed. He wore a black suit with a white dress shirt and a charcoal gray tie. He had black hair and always seemed to have a suntan.

"I will definitely let them know." Bishop noted. He then went back to Agents Townsend and Norman and said "I spoke to the chief. He's offered to send in his best people for this." he added in reference to the attempts to decipher the codes.

"I will relay that to my boss." Townsend began "I don't think that he will approve of it though." Agent Townsend had brown hair and brown eyes and was of average weight and of medium build. He wore gray suits, white dress shirts and black ties. He was entering his eighth year in the CIA. Agent Norman was also of average height and medium build. His suits were usually charcoal gray with matching ties and a white dress shirt. He was entering his tenth year at the agency, and was up for a promotion.

"It wouldn't surprise me though if he didn't." Bishop acknowledged.

Khalid Isawi arrived at his home which overlooked the farm just outside Jalalabad. He entered it and was greeted by his wife and children. Isawi then had a quick dinner and then announced "I need to be undisturbed for the next few hours as he excused himself from the table and walked over to the other side of the house where his private office was. Isawi entered his private office which was soundproof. It had two state of the art laptops and a desk in which his private papers were locked. The walls were gray and there was no window which helped protect his privacy. Khalid was the only one in his family who knew about the heroin and opium business that he has been conducting since the late 1990's. This secret was deliberately kept from the rest of his family who has been growing very suspicious for quite a while about how the family became suddenly very wealthy as well as the visitors who would visit the farm periodically. So far, Khalid was very successful in explaining it away while his family believed his every lie in the process. Khalid then took out his prepaid cellphone and placed a call to Ishmael Younis in Riyadh, Saudi Arabia. Younis quickly answered the call and asked "How are you my brother?"

"I am doing some paperwork." Khalid replied.

"It is time for you to make the sale." Younis ordered in reference to the complete divesture of Isawi's 100,000 shares of Cypress, Incorporated stock. Khalid knew that he was to immediately buy 500,000 shares of Pan Arabian Oil not only knowing how undervalued it was, but that the stock of Pan Arabian Oil was only hours away from skyrocketing in value. Khalid then ended the call and placed another one to their mutual broker Hans Gubioso who then asked "How can I help you Khalid?"

"I need to sell all of my shares of Cypress and reinvest every dollar from the sale into Pan Arabian Oil." Isawi requested.

"Consider it done." Gubioso replied as he sold the shares of Cypress that Khalid owned and reinvested them in Pan Arabian Oil. "The transaction has been completed. Is there anything else I can do for you?"

"That is all." Khalid said as he then hung up the phone. With that Khalid went to the al-Jazeera website and began to watch the live coverage of the Middle Eastern news network that was based out of Dubai.

9:45am

"How do you feel heading into the hearing Secretary Watson?" a Fox News reporter asked the Ohio Secretary of State. The clear blue skies and the blinding sun shone upon the Ohio State Supreme Court building in Columbus. The crisp November air gave the site an unusual aura. Most of those who were present were having trouble seeing due to the very illuminating sunlight which had been cast down upon the area. Outside the courthouse there were a crowd of reporters from every news agency possible.

"I am very confident that we can reach a resolution here in Ohio before the day is over." Eric Watson replied.

"What are your thoughts about the allegations of voter tampering?" a MSNBC reporter then inquired.

"I assure you these allegations are baseless." Watson shot back curtly. Meanwhile a reporter with false credentials was now waiting for a clear opening for the Ohio Secretary of State. He kept maneuvering his way around as well as through the various reporters who were mobbing Watson while peppering him with one question after another.

"Hey!' snarled one reporter.

"Watch it!" shot back another reporter as the reporter who was trying to get to Watson was brushing aside the others present. He kept staring at Watson the whole time.

"What will you do should your case for the GOP votes to be counted is shot down?" an ABC reporter asked while chiming in on the conversation.

"If we should lose this case then we will keep on fighting until the truth comes out." Watson said with a strong conviction in his voice.

"And what if the truth does come out that the votes were in fact actually tampered with?" a CBS reporter mused aloud waiting to discredit Watson. At the same time, the reporter with false credentials forced his way to Watson's right side, quickly pulled out his shiny black 357 Magnum and quickly pumped three shots into the head of the Ohio Secretary of State.

"Get him!" screamed the first reporter as he and everyone else quickly tackled the gunman. Another reporter then grabbed the gunman and put him into a headlock. He quickly snapped the gunman's neck back during the ensuing struggle between the reporters and the gunman.

"There's the signal!" Ayman al-Zawahiri stated to his men who were present "That is the cue to carry out the attack today!" he added as his voice now beamed with pride "Osama bin Laden's death will finally be avenged after all these years!"

"This brings back memories of the Ahmad Shah Massoud shooting!" Jabril Alawi observed "How monumental is this operation going to be today?"

"Let's just say that we will have won the battle by the end of the day." al-Zawahiri said confidentially.

"As in absolute victory over the infidels?" Khalid Isawi asked.

"What do you think?" al-Zawahiri asked with a sneer in his voice. He then got up from his chair and walked out of the room.

"Are you watching CNN?" Tim Lake asked Ian Daley.

"I just saw the shooting." Daley began "It is even more reason for you to beef up security at the Galleria! That was Massoud all over again!" he said in reference to the opposition leader of the Taliban being killed just two days before the September 11, 2001 attacks in New York and Washington.

"That was the first thought that crossed my mind." Lake responded "By the way if they do manage to let you go at Homeland Security, I think I can arrange to have an opening for Director of Mall Security waiting for you."

"I appreciate the offer, but I cannot allow someone to be fired just so I can be hired to take their place." Daley replied.

"The present director of security we have is so incompetent that he must be replaced." Lake began "I quizzed him on the security preparations for today and he was at best lackadaisical in answering them."

"I'm surprised that you still have him employed there after this morning," Daley replied.

"I cannot make a move until I speak to the owner and he is out of town until tonight." Lake said "His flight was cancelled due to that blizzard in the Pacific Northwest."

"Is there any way that you could relay orders to the lieutenant of the security in your mall?" Ian suggested.

"I already have been issuing orders to him since I suspended Bridges until further notice." Tim started "However there is no way that the lieutenant is ready to become director of security here. He has potential but he moved up the ranks very quickly and promoting him now would only put him way over his head."

"I see." Daley replied "Keep me posted."

"Was that our signal to proceed with the operation?" Hussein Ibrahim asked Saleh Bowadi as he watched the coverage of the shooting of the Ohio Secretary of State Eric Watson.

"Yes it was my brother!" Bowadi replied "It is time for us to get ready for our trip to Paradise." With that the two men began to prepare themselves for the assignment that they had been ordered to carry out.

"Mr. President, my men have been working on this since yesterday afternoon." the Director of Homeland Security Pat Ryan began "We cannot manage to figure out the kind of attack that they are planning on carrying out." The meeting was taking place in the Situation Room which is inside the White House. The oval desk was in the center of the room which displayed the latest state of the art computers along with the latest technology. It was these components which displayed the latest events that were unfolding throughout the world as well as the buildup, position and readiness of the militaries of every country in the world not to mention the same things going for every terrorist group known to mankind. However despite all these amenities that are at the disposal of the government as well as the intelligence agencies of the United States of America, they could not pinpoint a specific terrorist threat as of the present moment. Those who were present inside the Situation Room as well as those who are employed in the respective governmental and intelligence agencies which deals with the terrorist threats to national security were now feeling very perplexed over the strategies that were being used against them. Even the moment of the specific threat could not be pinpointed due to the secrecy that was being used by those who may be on the brink of carrying out a strike against the United States, its interests or even its allies. With everything factored in it has now become a source not only of frustration but of deep consternation as well.

"Your job is to prevent another terrorist attack from taking place. So far, all I have seen is once act of ineptitude after another from your department. If there is a terrorist attack carried out today, you will be out of a job. Do I make myself clear?" President Jeff Wolcott replied.

"How can I do my job if I have no leads to go on?" Ryan protested.

"Your responsibility is to utilize all of the resources that are available to you. I have yet to see any evidence of even one resource being utilized." Wolcott shot back "Your resignation is to be on my desk by noon."

"With all due respect Mr. President?" Director of National Intelligence Chet Jackson began "The man is trying to do his job, but there has been problems among those who work for the Department of Homeland Security."

"I guess a housecleaning is an order for Homeland." President Wolcott thought aloud.

"And this is why you're on the brink of losing the election. No one likes you as it is." Ryan thought as the Presidential Press Secretary entered the room "Ohio Secretary of State Eric Watson was seriously wounded in a shooting just now."

"Just what this country needs right now." Wolcott responded "We're going to have a political war on our hands. Has the assassin or assassins been arrested?"

"The lone gunman was killed during the ensuing struggle." the Press Secretary said.

"Sounds very suspicious to me." Agent Bishop said to Agent Downey in reference to the gunman dying in the ensuing struggle. The two had been watching the live coverage inside CIA Headquarters.

"Whoever killed him did so in order to silence him." Agent Downey responded

"I think there is something else going on." Bishop acknowledged.

"Any thinking person would feel the same way." Downey noted as the four agents were taking a coffee break in a break room at CIA Headquarters.

"It's obvious that the malls are going to be targeted I can tell you that much. Look at what today is." Bishop began "That is a no brainer! Look at what happened in Nairobi back in 2013 when the Westgate Mall was attacked!"

"Then why is nothing being done about it?" Downey inquired.

"That is the same question that I'm asking too." Bishop said while he rolled his eyes. Meanwhile Agents Townsend and Norman both entered the briefing room and Bishop then said "I think we may have received the signal that they intend to carry out an attack or attacks." as he pointed to the television screen.

"Just like Massoud!" Agent Townsend began as he and Agent Norman were watching live coverage of the Watson shooting "I think an attack is now imminent!"

"I don't think that they will wait two days to stike like they did on 9/11." Agent Norman reasoned "Today is Black Friday."

"We have been having that concern all day." Agent Downey began as Agent Bishop placed a call to FBI headquarters and informed his superiors about that was going on as well as the concerns that they were having.

"I'm informing my superiors!" Agent Townsend said as he placed a phone call to his immediate supervisor and told him what was going on. Meanwhile Agent Bishop got off the phone and said "Expect a phone call from Homeland Security very shortly. The wait did not last long as the call immediately came. Agent Townsend picked up the phone and said "Agent Townsend."

"Agent Townsend." began an official from the Department of Homeland Security "We just got a phone call from one of your superiors. He believes that the shooting of Eric Watson may be directly correlated to an impending terrorist attack."

"We are concerned that this was a similar signal that al-Qaeda sent out two days before the September 11, 2001 attacks when the opposition leader of the Taliban Massoud was gunned down just as he was giving an interview." Agent Townsend began as he then added "I will hand you the phone to Agent Bishop, he came up with that theory not me." Now Agent Townsend handed the phone to Agent Bishop who mouthed "Who is it?"

"Homeland Security for you." Agent Townsend replied while mouthing the words. Agent Bishop then said "Agent Bishop. How can I help you?"

"We just spoke to Agent Townsend and he says that you have a theory about a possible impending terrorist attack. We wish to hear your theory Agent Bishop." Art Graves from Homeland Security ordered.

"There is reason to believe that the shooting of Eric Watson may be a signal for al-Qaeda to carry out a terrorist relatively soon." Agent Bishop began.

"Would you care to tell us why you believe that this may be the case?" Graves inquired as he pressed on with the questioning.

"As everyone one knows, the opposition leader against the Taliban Ahmad Shah Massoud was killed just two days before the September 11th Attacks took place. Massoud was killed in order to prevent any opposition as well as giving the go ahead for the 9/11 attacks to take place. Today may very likely be a signal for al-Qaeda to carry out another attack against us very soon." Agent Bishop stated.

"I have a lot of trouble believing that." Graves began "I don't think that al-Qaeda would use the same signal to give the approval to carry out a terrorist attack."

"With all due respect, if we missed the signal the first time around then they would use that same signal again and again until we figure it out. However we figured it out the first time around and we never let on to al-Qaeda that we know about it.' Agent Bishop argued.

"I am afraid that we cannot rule the shooting of Ohio Secretary of State Eric Watson as a precursor for al-Qaeda to carry out an impending terrorist attack against us. We must look into this further before making a final decision about this." Art Graves noted.

"You are making a very serious mistake doing this. You must be aggressive about this lead." Agent Bishop implored Graves.

"Are you bullying me into following your lead?" Graves mused aloud.

"No I am worried that you make take too much time looking into this and that an attack may take place while Homeland Security is looking into whether this threat is credible or not. I am absolutely convinced that this threat is credible!" Agent Bishop shot back.

"Listen here Agent Bishop." Graves began "We receive millions of threats that come through the Department of homeland Security. May I remind you that almost all of them are hoaxes. Even the ones that we receive that are credible are quickly taken care of."

"You are taking this threat too lightly." Agent Bishop shot back.

"No! If anything you are taking this too seriously. You are reading into something that is not credible. Don't you ever accuse me or anyone in my department of taking terrorist threats too lightly. My men work twenty four hours a day seven days a week not to mention three hundred and sixty five days each year in order to keep the United States of America and for you to question my ability to properly do my job is the most irresponsible blatant thing you can do. How dare you question my patriotism you little weasel!" Graves exploded.

"No! You're the little weasel around here. You are too lazy to even look into a potential terrorist threat! Why don't you join the nearest al-Qaeda recruiting station? I am sure that they have room for a moron like you!" Bishop bellowed.

"I will be talking to your superior officer." Graves snarled.

"Actually I am in the process of contacting your superior officer you moron." Bishop ripped as Graves slammed the phone.

"What happened just now?" Agent Downey inquired.

"That idiot refused to look into this tip." Agent Bishop exploded "I thought that the Department of Homeland Security was supposed to prevent terrorist attacks, not bring about another one due to their incompetence."

"I know someone you can talk to." Agent Townsend began "Ian Daley."

"And why didn't you say so earlier?" Agent Bishop snarled.

"Because I thought that Ian Daley would be the one calling you. This is his function at Homeland Security." Agent Townsend said as he called Ian Daley's cellphone. Daley picked it up and said "Daley speaking."

"Ian, it's me Agent Townsend from the CIA." He began "We just phoned in a tip to your department and some moron refused to take it seriously.'

"I am afraid that I was the last person in the Department of Homeland Security who actually took their job seriously.' Daley replied.

"Was?" Townsend mused "What happened?"

"The clowns sent me home because I tried to warn them of a specific threat and they didn't take it seriously." Ian replied.

"And what was the threat?" Townsend asked.

"The malls may be attacked just like the one in Nairobi, Kenya during the autumn of 2013. They could use the same methods like the terrorists who carried out the massacre and hostage taking in Mumbai, India this time back in 2008." Daley recalled. "The shooting of Eric Watson further validated the possibility that this may occur as soon as today."

"Agent Bishop just got off the phone with someone from Homeland Security. He mentioned that very same theory about Watson's shooting being a go ahead for the attacks to occur." Townsend added.

"I think that it is time for us to go to work." Ian Daley began.

"I agree." Agent Townsend noted "Just how do we go rogue?"

"Leave that up to me." Ian said as he added "Just tip off your superiors that this may be one threat scenario that may occur as the day continues on."

"My brother." began Sheikh Jabril Alawi as he spoke to Ishmael Younis "The politician has been eliminated." Alawi said in reference to Eric Watson "We now await our brothers to strike the infidels.'

"I am glad that everything is moving smoothly so far." Younis replied in reference to the impending operation that would be carried out against the Americans. He then inquired "Have you sold your holding in Cypress yet?"

"I am about to?" Alawi said as he then added "Did you want me to wait?"

"Yes, wait until just before ten o'clock this evening. That is when the operation is scheduled to begin. He then asked "So have you heard from Khalid as of late?" he inquired in reference to Khalid Isawi.

"Yes." Alawi started as he continued on "He is going to meet with some friends in Columbia next week. They are on the brink of expanding their business to include Khalid's farm."

"This is very good news." Ishmael said. "The best thing we could do was to ally ourselves with the drug cartels."

"I agree." Jabril began "At least we have enough sense to infiltrate them and not to make it obvious that we are trying to take out their best customers." Sheikh Alwai noted as the conversation came to a close. Sheikh Alwai had been raised in a secular Islamic environment in Jidda, Saudi Arabia during his formative years during the 1970's. His life began to change forever when the Grand Mosque was seized in Mecca on November 20, 1979. After the takeover came to a bloody and violent end, Saudi Arabia began to incorporate Wahhabi Islam in every facet of the nation. Jabril Ilawi at first resisted the change sensing that it was too radical, but after the Soviet invasion of Afghanistan, his views changed when he befriended Osama bin Laden who convinced him to accept the Wahhabi practice of Islam. Alawi fought with bin Laden in Afghanistan and was among the earliest members of al-Qaeda. However Osama bin Laden suggested that Alawi would be best suited as a fund raiser for al-Qaeda while working for a Saudi securities brokerage firm. Alwai raised millions of dollars through al-Qaeda while maintaining the terror networks investments at the same time. This was done while working for The Ibn Saud Brokerage House as an investment banker. Alawi was able to make many contacts in the financial industry both domestic and abroad. Those contacts would come in very handy through the years. Alawi was able to receive insider information on occasion and knew when to act on it without being detected. Alawi would make annual payments to the Saudi courts in exchange for escaping prosecution. All in all, the alliance between al-Qaeda, the financial industry as well as the drug cartels would prove to become a match that was made in heaven. Each hand would wash the other and things ran very smoothly knowing that each party carried out their affairs very discreetly without alerting law enforcement. This is how all parties involved has been able to escape detection for as long as they have. On this day, the alliance would be on the brink of completing their biggest operation ever.

"I need to take a break." Irene Daley said to her sister Irma "My feet are starting to hurt."

"My footsies need some rest anyways." Irma replied as the two began to look for a bench inside the Galleria Mall. They found a bench which was in front of the fountain near the main food court. The twins quickly sat down and began to relax for a little while "I can't get over how crowded it is here." Irma noted as she saw the thongs of shoppers who were buying Christmas gifts for their family and friends.

"Mom always told us how crowded it gets at the malls on Black Friday." Irene replied.

"We've heard the stories, but have never got an appreciation for it until now." Irma added as she then changed the subject "I miss Mom."

"Same here." Irene replied "The holidays have never really been the same since 9/11."

"I think this is the most into it I have been since she was killed." Irma acknowledged.

"I feel the same way." Irene noted "I'm so glad that we met 'Alexis and Andi.' in reference to another set of twins who they met at Syracuse University back in August. They had lost their mother in the September 11th attacks and taught their new friends how to live once more. Just then they noticed someone standing in front of them. They quickly looked up and actually saw a couple of people "Josh, Brodie?" Irene gasped. Both young men wore black and gray hooded sweatshirts from Hollister. They had blue jeans on and wore black and purple Baltimore ravens knit hats. They were both clean shaven with reddish blond hair for Josh and light brown hair for Brodie.

"Irene, Irma?" Josh replied.

"Yes, it's us. You two act like you haven't seen us in ages.' Irma replied.

"We haven't seen you since August. I didn't recognize both of you until I heard your voices and it took us a moment to pick up on it." Brodie noted "This has to be the happiest I have seen you in years!"

"We both met another set of twins at the 'Cuse. They lost their mother on 9/11 too and taught us how to live again!" Irene said enthusiastically.

"Is this awesome or what!" Irma noted.

"Let's hang out!" Josh suggested.

"We can start by you sitting with us for a little while." Irene began "Out footsies are sore. We've been at this since eleven last night!" With that Josh and Brodie sat down with Irene and Irma and the two caught up for a while.

"Do you think Daley was right after all?" Reggie Patterson asked Harvey Harrison in reference to Daley mentioning that the assassination of Massood as a precursor to the 9/11 attacks. The two men were meeting in Harrison's office.

"How can we be sure what to do if we don't have a specific threat to deal with?" Harrison shot back "Besides our resources are stretched as it is."

"I think Daley is on to something." Patterson acknowledged "The assassination of Massood was a signal for the attacks to be carried out on September 11th. Today's assassination of the Ohio Secretary of State may indicate that an attack is imminent."

"So when does the attack take place? Two days from now? Two hours from now? Even two minutes from now? No one is certain that there is a direct correlation between the shooting of Eric Watson and an impending terrorist attack. If this two day rule were to hold true, then the terrorists would be quickly caught and there would be no attack occurring. Think Reggie think! We must think like they think. They would not be stupid enough to carry out an attack on Sunday at the NFL stadiums. These men want to strike us. They would never use the two day rule knowing that we would be on to it!"

"But they would use the shoot a high profile official as a signal." Patterson noted "Osama bin Laden had his al-Qaeda network do so just before 9/11. I think we need Daley to return here at once."

"We don't need Daley back here anyways. The man was too brash for us anyways. He was beginning to become a major headache for us. We already have enough problems here as it is. We don't need any more issues that will weigh us down even further."

"Welcome." the security guard at the United States Capital Building said to both Dick Tilden and Irving Rosenberg. They showed their credentials to the security guard and were then searched extensively as Rosenberg said would happen to the two. Once they were finished, they were now escorted by another guard to the holding room where they would wait to be called to testify before the congressional committee. Once they entered the holding room the guard now said "Please help yourselves to some coffee, tea, orange juice, bagels or cereal. I know that it has been a long flight for you."

"Thank you." Tilden and Rosenberg replied as they now helped themselves to a bagel as well as a bowl of cereal while sipping on some orange juice.

Once the guard left the two alone, Rosenberg asked "How are you feeling?"

"I am very nervous going into this." Tilden replied.

"That is to be expected." Rosenberg replied "I have to ask this question before we continue. It is my job to do so. Please don't take this personally, but have you told me everything you know about what Barton and the voting machines."

"Yes." Tilden replied emphatically while staring Rosenberg directly in the eyes while answering his question.

"That is all I wanted to know. You are going to do just fine in there." Rosenberg stated.

11:00am

"Raise your right hand and repeat after me. I, Richard Wayne Tilden do solemnly swear." The Sergeant at Arms began.

"I, Richard Wayne Tilden do solemnly swear." Tilden replied.

"That I will tell this committee the truth, the whole truth and nothing but the truth so help me God." The Sergeant at Arms concluded.

"That I will tell this committee the truth, the whole truth and nothing but the truth so help me God." Tilden responded as he completed his oath to the congressional committee.

"Is your name Richard Wayne Tilden?" Congressman Robards began as the Robards commission was now questioning its second witness for the day.

"Yes sir." Tilden replied.

"And are you the founder and Chief Executive officer of Cypress, Incorporated which is based in Miami, Florida?"

"Yes sir." Tilden replied.

"With that I would like to remind you that you are under oath at this time." Robards said.

"Yes sir." Tilden acknowledged.

"Please state for the committee about Cypress, incorporated and the services that they offer?" Congressman Robards now inquired.

"Cypress Incorporated is a technological and internet company which offers computerized machinery as well as internet services for the purpose of making life easier for the public." Tilden replied.

"Does your company offer voting machines as one of the products that Cypress produces?" Roberts than asked.

"Yes." Tilden started "We offer voting machines to municipalities."

"When did you begin to offer voting machines and what motivated Cypress, Incorporated to offer voting machines as a product?"

"First of all we began to offer voting machines as a product after seven years of conducting research into what had been a potential product line. This product line was first discussed at the onset of the 2000 presidential recount. We were concerned about the voting procedures in Florida at the time and Cypress, incorporated felt that it had an obligation to prevent another voting debacle from happening. That is what led us to create the voting machines that have been used in the past two presidential elections." Tilden explained while continuing on "By offering what was considered to be a foolproof product that another voting debacle would be averted. However in this case Cypress is now embroiled in such a debacle."

"Did you or anyone else have any prior knowledge of any tampering of the votes for the November 6 presidential election of this year?" Congressman Robards now asked. He continued to be in the process of positioning himself for a presidential bid four years from now.

"Never." Tilden replied.

"Did you have any prior knowledge of any of your employees carrying out the act of voter tampering?" Robards inquired while going for the knockout.

"I had no prior knowledge of any of my employees engaging in voter tampering before the election took place. However, after the election we began to suspect a certain employee during an internal investigation. His work performance had been questionable leading up to Election Day. We had no choice but to relegate him to desk work and ultimately a paid leave of absence while deciding whether he should continue on with his employment at Cypress, Incorporated." Tilden answered.

"And what activities have this certain employee engaged in?" Robards now asked in a rapid fire fashion.

"You would have to ask Ian Daley. He is employed by the Department of Homeland Security department." Tilden shot back.

"You mean to tell me that I must ask an employee of the Department of Homeland Security to answer the question that I have just asked you." Robards surmised.

"Yes that would be correct given the fact that national security is on the line." Tilden shot back while staggering Robards with the zinger of a response which now left the ten term congressman from Texas feeling very dazed and confused.

"I need to confer with my fellow members of the committee before we decide whether to continue on with my examination." Robards said as he now summoned the committee members for a group conference "What do you recommend I do?" Robards inquired. He was in desperate need of advice and fast. Never before as a trial lawyer that he had to deal with a bombshell of this magnitude not to mention the fact that it dealt with national security.

"We need to summon Ian Daley to testify at once." Congressman Killian replied "Given the fact that this pertains to national security that it would be appropriate for a member of the Department of Homeland Security to be summoned to testify."

"Congressman Killian is right." Congressman Yates began "We could be opening a can of worms unless we summon Daley to testify."

"This is exactly what I was concerned about when the Patriot Act was debated in this building back in 2002." Congressman Martinez of New Mexico added.

"How long would it take to draw up a summons for Ian Daley to come here and testify?" Robards quickly asked.

"I would say a few hours." Congressman Martinez began and he quickly added before Robards could get another jab in "First we must inform the congressional legal department of our intention to summon Ian Daley to come here and testify. Then once we explain to the legal department the reason that we are summoning Ian Daley to testify before this committee that it could take another two hours to draw up such a summons given the circumstances that it is being written under. We could very well be looking at Monday afternoon at the very earliest that Daley would be able to receive the summons. We must call this hearing into recess and order Dick Tilden and his legal counsel to remain here until Ian Daley testifies before this committee."

"Does anyone else agree with Congressman Martinez's assessment before I inform Dick Tilden of our decision?" Robards now asked.

"Yes." they replied one by one.

"Alright then." Robards acknowledged as the committee members returned to their seats. He then said "We are going to be in recess until Ian Daley testifies before this committee. I advise that you and Mr. Rosenberg are to remain in town until Ian Daley is able to verify what you have just told me."

"Yes sir.' Tilden and Rosenberg replied in unison.

"This committee is adjourned until Mr. Ian Daley is present to testify." Robards stated as the hearing was adjourned until further notice.

"Well it looks like we are going to be stuck here for the weekend." Irving Rosenberg said.

"You told me to tell the whole truth." Tilden replied.

"You did the right thing." Rosenberg noted as the two now began to leave the Capital Building "Listen we are not to answer a single question from the media until I tell you otherwise." Rosenberg said as he prepared Tilden for the media onslaught that the two would face momentarily. Once they arrived at the lobby, a crush of reporters converged on the two. One by one they were peppering both men with questions in rapid fire succession.

"What threat to national security do we face at this hour?" one reporter asked.

"No comment." Rosenberg replied as he and Tilden were racing out of the building.

"Are under an imminent threat of a terrorist attack at this hour?" another reporter inquired.

"I said no comment." Rosenberg replied almost coldly.

"What does the Department of Homeland Security have to do with this presidential recount?" a third reporter now mused aloud in hopes of throwing off the two.

"No comment." Rosenberg stated as they were now outside the Capital while members of the Capital security force were barricading the press from both Tilden as well as Rosenberg. They now raced to a nearby taxi and they took off for a secluded hotel where they would not be disturbed until they were recalled to continue on with their testimony before the Robards Committee.

"We can now confirm the reports that Ohio Secretary of State Eric Watson has died of his wounds suffered from the shooting outside the State Supreme Court Building in Columbus almost two hours ago." the MSNBC reporter announced.

"This has to be the signal." Ian Daley said to Tim Lake as Lake had called Daley only moments earlier for advice about how to deal with a potential threat "You must call in the local police, sheriff as well as the state troopers about it."

"I already have." Lake noted "I was calling you about how to do this ethically. I know you are a by the book person who is not afraid to think outside the box."

"Just keep doing what you're doing" Ian began "The fact that you're consulting with me is a good thing. It's better to be safe than sorry."

"I would rather take the extra precautions than live with a tragedy." Tim acknowledged.

"That is always the best thing to do." Daley began as he then added "The chatter that we have been picking up on was the same pattern that took place leading up to 9/11. I am convinced that they may soon carry out an attack against us."

"I feel the same way." Lake started "Just why are we the only ones who are convinced that the malls will be among the targets." he then mused.

"It has to be the day that it is." Ian claimed "Besides I now have a few people in both the FBI and the CIA who agree with me on this."

"I am already preparing for such a scenario. The holiday season has always given us the jitters since September 11th." Tim stated "The stress level has always been at its highest during the Christmas season, but 9/11 has only made it worse."

"How do you manage it?" Daley asked.

"It isn't easy, but we get through it every year." Lake noted "How do you cope with your job 365 days a year?"

"I handle it the same way. I just get through it day by day." Ian began "Although I think my days at Homeland Security are numbered though.

"The job offer at the Galleria still stands." Tim said.

"If I am let go at Homeland, I will take you up on it." Daley responded.

"I think my footsies are ready to walk again." Irene began.

"Same here." Irma replied "Wanna join us." she then asked Josh and Brodie.

"We would be glad to." Josh replied. He and Brodie then joined the Daley twins as they resumed their holiday shopping "So how did you meet your two new friends?" he mused while changing the subject.

"We met at an off campus party." Irene began "We were just sitting there and these other two sets of twins came up to us and said 'Isn't it ironic that there are another set of twins at the same house party. How often does that happen?' They began to talk to us. We were withdrawn in the beginning, but they quickly drew us out of our shells."

"I see." Brodie started "This is the most outgoing we have ever seen you two."

"We know." Irma smiled "Mom's death took so much out of us for years. Alexis and Andi brought us both out of our depression. They taught us never to let the terrorists win."

"We must never let them win." Josh noted "That is exactly one of the goals that they wish to achieve is to have everyone live in fear and sadness."

"We have definitely resolved to take back our lives." Irene stated.

"Everyone will be glad that you two decided to do so." Brodie added.

"Mr. President." began the press secretary "Eric Watson's dead."

"They will definitely try to pin this on us." President Wolcott replied "I know that they are hopping mad about this recount. It's obvious that Governor Freeman's campaign has been tampering with the votes."

"By the way, you have a visitor." the press secretary started "He has some information that you need to know. It may change your thoughts about the election."

"Bring him in." Wolcott ordered gruffly.

"Mr. President." began Frank Carter who was an investigative reporter for *The Washington Post* "Thank you for having me come in." Carter had a receding gray hairline and wore his trademark black suit and dark blue tie and white dress shirt. His bifocals gave him a distinguished look. One that was very befitting given his many years as a reporter who worked the Washington, DC political beat. The ace reporter looked much shaken up. This was very rare given the fact that hardly anything would shake the unflappable reporter known for his cool, calm composure.

"Have a seat Frank." President Wolcott replied "How can I help you?"

"*The Washington Post* is on the brink of running a story that there has been voter tampering in the election, but it wasn't from the Freeman campaign."

"Then who was it from?" Wolcott then inquired.

"It looks like it may have originated by someone who is affiliated with your party by the looks of things." Carter noted.

"That's preposterous!" the president gasped "There is no way that my party would partake in such a thing."

"The evidence does point in that direction." Carter continued "I can hold off on running the story until you conduct an internal investigation. If you refuse to do so, then the American people will think that you were in on it."

"Are you blackmailing me?" Wolcott then asking in an accusatory tone.

"No I am only trying to be responsible." Carter added.

"Blackmail is among the most irresponsible of activities out there." President Wolcott snarled.

"You have a chance to prove that you have no prior knowledge of this." Carter said giving the president an opening.

"If any of my people were in fact involved in voter tampering then they would be out of a job immediately and prosecuted to the fullest extent of the law!" the president shot back.

"Then do the investigation." Carter implored.

"And that I will do!" Wolcott stated. With that Frank Carter left the Oval Office and headed to his car. Frank Carter had first begun working for *The Washington Post* just days before the break in at the Watergate hotel back in 1972. Since then the Des Moines, Iowa native had become the chief political correspondent for the only newspaper he has ever worked for. Frank first became employed as a cub reporter while he attended Georgetown University. *The Washington Post* was so impressed with his work that he became a full time worker after his graduation. Carter worked under legendary reporters such as Carl Bernstein and Bob Woodward. Frank learned so much while working with the two men as well as Ben Bradlee and George Will. This experience helped Carter immensely as he first made a name for himself during the Iran-Contra scandal. Carter would also be instrumental in later scandals such as Gary Hart's affair with Donna Rice that derailed the former's 1988 presidential bid after he emerged as the front runner. Carter's best work came in from the mid-1990's through the late 2000's. Among his legendary moments included Whitewater, the Monica Lewinsky Affair, the 2000 Florida Recount, the handling of the Iraq War in 2003 as well as the Abu Gharib incident. Carter was also known for his scathing exposes of the George W. Bush administration, Blackwater, the 2008 Financial Crisis and John Edwards affair with Rielle Hunter. Although the 2010's were a decade in which Carter took a step back and battled a myriad of health problems including a heart attack and a battle with cancer which had long since been in remission, Carter always found time to mentor young reports as he had once been mentored by luminaries such as Bernstein, Woodward, Bradlee and Will. Carter never forgot how much he learned from the aforementioned reports and this was the other way he could repay them besides retaining what he learned from them and giving a quality story every time. Carter now drove away with the realization that the other stories which he was made famous for may dwarf in comparison given the story that he may soon break.

"Well Mr. President." the presidential press secretary began "What are you going to do about this?" Evelyn was sixty years old and had light brown hair which was beginning to show gray. Her blue eyes were covered with brown glasses. She was always elegantly dressed in light colored pantsuits with multi-colored dress shirts. She was short and petite at 4'11" and eighty pounds. Despite her appearance, Evelyn could be very intimidating when she had to be.

"I have no idea. This is such a shock to me. How can anyone be so stupid? I'm not sure if this is even true for that matter." President Wolcott said as he was feeling very shell shocked over the news.

"You know what to do Mr. President." she then added "You must do it no matter how hard it is for you to do. You heard what Carter threatened to do."

"But I would never ever authorize such a thing." Wolcott added.

"I believe you." she began "Just conduct the internal investigation just so you can clear your name." the presidential press secretary implored Wolcott.

"Alright." Wolcott relented "I will have the attorney general do it. Please summon him here at once."

"Yes Mr. President." the press secretary said as she then summoned Attorney General Stevens to the Oval Office.

"Agent Townsend." Ian Daley began "I alerted my friend who manages the Galleria Mall. He is in the process of alerting the other malls who are managed by the Samson Property Group about this potential threat."

"I am glad to hear it." Agent Townsend replied "I am going to have you talk to the person who made this possible connection." As he motioned Agent Bishop to the phone. He handed the phone to Agent Bishop and said "I have a friend who would like to talk to you."

"Alright." Bishop mouthed as he added "He better not be like Graves."

"Trust me, he is the complete opposite." Townsend responded.

"Hello Agent Bishop." He said.

"Agent Bishop I'm Ian Daley from Homeland Security. Agent Townsend told me about your theory and what Graves put you through. There was no excuse for Graves to do what he did. I have had problems with him since I first met him. The man should have never gone into governmental service." Ian started "In fact Homeland Security sent me home because

I voiced concern that they were taking this potential terrorist threat too lightly. I mentioned that the malls may be attacked and I was completely ignored as though I was talking to a brick wall."

"That is exactly how I felt today as well." Agent Bishop began "I thought that the function of the Department of Homeland Security was to prevent terrorist attacks from occurring now enabling them to happen."

"Those are exactly my thoughts as well right now Agent Bishop. I have alerted the Samson Property Group about this. I am also in the process of sending out an alert about this to the President."

"I heard that Wolcott is as dumb as a brick as well when it comes to these kinds of things." Agent Bishop noted.

"It doesn't hurt to try though. We cannot afford to leave any stone unturned especially right now when the lives of tens of millions of Americans may be at stake."

"It's time." Hussein Ibrahim said to Saleh Bowadi in reference for the mission that they were about to carry out.

"I'm ready." Saleh responded. The two men left their apartment and slowly walked over to Hussein's car.

"The traffic jam will be worse later." Hussein began "So we're leaving now."

"We must split up once we enter the mall." Saleh began "and do some shopping. We have to blend in with the other shoppers. If they see us together beforehand then the operation is over before it begins." The two got into the 2007 blue Ford Aspire and Hussein began to put the key in the ignition key "Soon we will be in Paradise."

"I am looking forward to it." Bowadi noted.

"I feel the same way." Ibrahim grinned.

It was nightfall over Afghanistan. Khalid Isawi was in his private office which was on the other side of his home. Alawi was now surfing the internet checking out the latest developments in the Middle East. He knew better than to go on the CNN, FOX News or the MSNBC website to check out the latest news knowing that it could be traced back to him once the attacks take place. Isawi's cellphone rang. He quickly picked it up and said "Hello."

"My brother." Sheikh Jabril Alawi began "I think you should know that the meeting in Columbia is still on for next week. Our client is very interested in completing the deal then."

"We need to be aggressive in convincing them that we have the best offer." Isawi noted "We definitely need their business in order to have enough of a cash infusion for our next venture. Their accepting our offer will be enough for it to happen."

"The sooner we get their business, the sooner we can commence the new business venture." Alawi added knowing the urgency in completing the deal with the Columbian drug cartel. Meanwhile they were waiting for the operation to commence within hours from now. They were following the news on al-Jazeera waiting for the strike to take place.

Meanwhile Jabril was waiting for ten o'clock to be on the horizon so he could dump his shares of Cypress stock along with the other al-Qaeda operatives who were also waiting to conduct the same transaction just before the attacks were to begin.

"What do you think about the expansion of the fields?" Isawi began as he changed the subject.

"Anything that will help business would be wonderful right about now. We cannot afford to sit on the sidelines and watch our competitors make inroads against us." Alawi acknowledged.

"That we must not allow to happen." Isawi added as the watch continued.

12:45pm

"The Robards Commission has suddenly adjourned this morning after a bombshell took place during the testimony of Cypress Owner and CEO Dick Tilden said that although he had no prior knowledge before the election that one of his employees may have tampered with the voting machines in Ohio, Pennsylvania, Florida, Virginia and Arizona, he was first made aware of that possibility a day after Election Day. It was when Dick Tilden was asked the extent of the investigation of the employee who was being investigated and he said that to answer the question would become a violation of national security. As a result, a member of the Department of Homeland Security who handled the complaint will now be summoned to testify before the Robards Commission early next week." The CNN reporter announced as he now broke the news regarding the latest developments in the investigation into voter tampering involving Cypress, Incorporated by the Robards Commission."

"I need to speak to Ian Daley at once." Harvey Harrison said to Reggie Patterson.

"He handled this complaint didn't he?" Patterson mused aloud.

"Correct." Harrison began "First I will need to speak to the legal department before I speak to Ian."

"Harvey, the briefing is about to take place." Reggie noted.

"This should only take a moment." Harrison said as he quickly placed a call to the legal department. "Look, I need you to help me about . . ."

"Would this regard the testimony that Dick Tilden just gave to the Robards Committee?" a lawyer for the legal department surmised.

"Yes." Harrison said.

"Let us look into it and we will call you back within an hour or two at the latest." the lawyer said as he ended the call. Harvey Harrison now walked briskly to the conference room where the meeting was going to take place and commenced it immediately.

"What is the latest about the terrorist threat?" Harrison asked.

"We are still perplexed about where the threat is coming from." Art Graves replied.

"Excuse me." Bart Quincy began "Ian Daley is so convinced that they are going to strike at the malls that he is in the process of alerting all of the nation's malls about such a threat." Bart Quincy was the youngest employee at Ridgemont at the age of 25. His wore brown wire rimmed glasses, had a mop of brown curly hair and a day's growth of stubble. He was of medium height and build and he usually wore a denim shirt and tan khaki slacks.

"Daley is going over my head on this!" Harrison exploded "Bad enough I just consulted our legal department about how to handle him being implicated in Dick Tilden's testimony to the Robards Commission and now this! Daley needs to go!"

"I think it would be best for everyone here if he was not allowed to continue on here." Reggie Patterson acknowledged.

"What if a terrorist attack does occur?" Quincy began "How would you feel about letting him go once it comes out that he was actually right about this terrorist threat once and for all?"

"Always got to be the rebel around here." Art Graves snarled.

"And you're the one who always has to be the moron of the group, but I see that you have some company this afternoon when it comes to being one." Quincy shot back.

"That will be enough." Harrison said sternly "We are here to discuss how to prevent a terrorist threat and not to engage in infighting. Does anyone in here have a clue about the threat that we are facing?"

"None." those present said almost in unison.

"Well keep on trying until you come up with something." Harrison ordered "And no one is to leave here until this threat is deciphered once and for all. Do I make myself clear?"

"Yes." they replied and then left the conference room in order to decipher the threat.

"I guess that we are going to have to leave a little earlier to get our weapons and vests." Hussein Ibrahim began as they parked in a secluded area of the mall. It was a little farther than the two had planned to park. They walked into the Galleria at a leisurely pace in order to be unable to be detected. The walk lasted a few minutes until they entered the mall. Once they entered the mall Salah then asked "We'll meet at 1:30?"

"See you then." Ibrahim replied as the two separated and began to walk around the mall. Hussein quickly found Macy's and began to look over the pots and pans.

"Is there anything I can help you with?" a female clerk in her mid-twenties asked.

"I'm trying to find some pots and pans for my mom as a Christmas gift. Is there a special brand that you would recommend?" Hussein inquired.

"I can show you our most durable brand." she replied. The young woman then led Ibrahim to the brand. He looked them over and decided to buy them.

"I'll take them." Ibrahim responded.

"I can cash you out right over there." the young woman said as Hussein followed her over to the cash register. She told Hussein the total and he handed her the cash. Once she gave him the change, the young woman then said "Thank you and Happy Holidays."

"You're welcome and Happy Holidays to you too." Ibrahim replied as he then thought *"It won't be a Happy Holiday much longer."* as he walked out of Macy's. Hussein was now marveled at the huge crowd that was turning out at the Galleria Mall. This was exactly what he and Saleh were hoping for. The idea of such a high body could would not only please him and Saleh, but Ayman al-Zawahiri and Allah as well. The conditions for carrying out an attack of such a large magnitude were more than ideal. This was a perfect scenario for al-Qaeda.

"So where are we going to shop next?" Irene Daley asked Irma.

"I don't know about you, but I am beginning to feel very tired." Irma replied as they were deciding about where they were going to have their lunch. The twins were checking out the restaurants as well as the lines for each one in the food court. They were now discussing their choices for which line they would like to wait in.

"I would like to wait at the Taco Bell line, but it is going to be a while." Irene suggested.

"It looks like Burger King has the shortest line here." Irma acknowledged.

"I think that would be a good idea." Irene acknowledged as the two began to walk over to the line at Burger King.

At the same time, Saleh Bowadi was now at the food court waiting in the same Burger King line. He was amazed at the long lines for customers who were waiting to eat their lunch. He had no question that this was going to be a great day. He had been waiting in line for almost twenty minutes and he was now more than halfway to placing his order. Soon the line would begin to make quicker when another cashier took to her station. Within minutes Saleh placed his order for some chicken tenders and bottled water.

"That guy up there." Irene said in reference to Saleh while leaning over to Irma and said "I'm suspicious of him."

"Same here." Irma replied as the old wounds from their mother's death began to come back in a torrent.

"I know it's hard for you to believe but if he had a shopping bag and looser clothing, I would be suspicious of him as well." a man who was standing behind the twins replied.

"We lost our mother when the Pentagon was attacked on 9/11." Irene replied.

"I am so sorry to hear that." the middle aged man replied "I understand why you would think this way. The malls are well secured. If they were going to attack a mall, believe me they would have done it before this year." Now the Daley twins were beginning to feel a little more at ease about Saleh.

Bowadi then waited another few minutes before he received his order. He quickly consumed what would be his last meal while walking over to make a quick purchase at Sears. Once he bought some clothes he began to carry the bag to Hussein's car. Just as Saleh was arriving at the car, Hussein was just steps away from him. He leaned over the Saleh and said "It's time." Bowadi nodded and said "Let's get ready."

With that they put their packages in the car and began to put on their suicide vests without being detected. Once they had everything in place, they reached over and took out another couple of long plastic shopping bags. Inside those bags were the AK-47's that they would use to carry out the attacks. They looked at the time and realized that they were minutes away from carrying out their jihad against the American people.

"Dan." Dick Tilden began "I apologize for not reaching you sooner, but things has been very hectic since the testimony this morning."

"I was watching it on CNN." Dan Merkel replied "How long do you think that you will be sequestered up there?"

"I am afraid that we will have to remain up here until Monday or Tuesday at the very earliest." Tilden acknowledged as he then added "Until then this is your show. Don't let me down."

"I promise I won't let you down." Merkel replied.

"Dick." Irving Rosenberg began "I need to speak to Dan immediately." Tilden then handed his cellphone to Rosenberg who began his conversation with Merkel "Dan, I need to know if you have been completely truthful with Dick. Have you?"

"Of course I have been completely honest." Merkel replied "It's that legal department and the law enforcement agencies that have been making things extremely difficult."

“That is all I needed to know. Thank you.” Rosenberg started as he then said “Dick would you like to say anything else to Dan?”

“No.” Dick replied while he nodded his head side to side. Rosenberg then hung up the phone and said “I believe Dan.”

“So do I.” Tilden noted.

“Mr. President.” Chief of Staff Jones began “They have decided to postpone the hearing in Ohio until Monday.” Jones was 6'6" and weighed 240 pounds. He had light brown hair and green eyes. He usually wore light suits and ties in the spring and summer, but switched to dark suits and ties during the winter while his white dress shirts were the only constant year round. At the age of fifty five, the chief of staff was known as the stabilizing influence as well as the steady guiding force in the Wolcott Administration.

“I see.” President Wolcott replied “I am concerned that Watson’s death could result in the court’s ruling for Freeman out of sympathy for Watson’s assassination.

“I don’t think the courts would ever be that stupid. I think you would make a strong case for the public though.” Jones noted.

“The judges are members of the public. They have always been private citizens well before they became judges.” President Wolcott stated.

“Remember Mr. President, the judges make their decision by rule of law, not by political affiliation.” the chief of staff preached.

"Have you forgotten the conservative justices of the Supreme Court who ruled in favor of George W. Bush in *Bush v. Gore* back in December 2000?" Wolcott recalled "Gore had that election won. That ruling forever changed the course of America history and it was for the worse!"

"Sir, I am sure that the rule of law played a considerable role in their decision." Chief of Staff Jones began "Of course I would like to believe that."

"But that is now what really happened." Wolcott began "Both you know it and I know it. I know that you would still like to believe that there is an America where the rule of law is a guiding factor when it comes to making judicial decisions but that is not how it always works. Any judge is vulnerable to being influenced by political or non-political favors in order to make a decision regardless of who they are. Even the Supreme Court in not immune to that. Look at what happened back in 2000. Need I say more?"

"I guess not." Jones responded as he threw his hands up in the air and walked out of the Oval Office.

"You wish to see me Mr. President." Attorney General Hugh Stevens said as soon as he entered the Oval Office. The Attorney General was always dressed in dark Armani suits, white dress shirts and dark silk ties. He was sixty one years old and was the former governor of California.

"Hugh, please sit down." President Wolcott began as Stevens quickly sat down. Wolcott then continued "Frank Carter stopped by here earlier this morning. He claims that persons connected to us may have tampered with the votes just to make the Freeman campaign look bad."

"That is preposterous!" Attorney General Stevens gasped.

"Carter has said that he will break the story in Sunday's edition of the Post unless we conduct an internal investigation into this matter." Wolcott noted.

"I think this is blackmail." Stevens said "Giving into him means that we may have something to hide."

"What do you suggest we do?" Wolcott then asked.

"I say we think it over, call your advisors as well as the cabinet in for an emergency meeting. We will discuss this and then make a final decision tonight." Stevens explained.

"What do you think I should do?" President Wolcott inquired.

"I would tell Carter to publish the story." Stevens began.

"Publish the story?" Wolcott blurted.

"Let me finish." Stevens said while motioning Wolcott to be quiet "If we tell Carter to publish the story the public will be outraged, but it will mean that we have nothing to hide. It will get you off the hook." the Attorney General reasoned.

"I want my advisors and the cabinet to hear your argument." Wolcott started "I will summon them here at once."

"I wonder if this is true." Frank Carter mused as he was thinking about how far the reaching the voter controversy really was. "*There was no way that this could even be possible.*" Carter thought knowing that a member of the Department of Homeland Security could now be asked to testify to the Robards Commission about his knowledge of a potential terrorist threat. "*Could terrorism be somehow connected to voter tampering? Only Hollywood or a novelist could dream of something of this magnitude. There is no way that this could even be real or could it?*" he wondered as he now began to place a call to the editor who quickly answered the call. Carter then said "There is a possibility that we may have to add a lot more to the story that I was planning on breaking Sunday"

"How more could you be adding to the story?" the editor inquired.

"I am afraid it will be much more than I previously envisioned." Carter responded.

"How huge is the bombshell that you have or may have discovered?" he wondered aloud.

"I can't discuss it over the phone, but all I can say is that only a Hollywood movie or someone like Tom Clancy would dream up something like this." Frank stated.

"Let me know when you call tell me about this new development." the editor said.

"I will." Carter replied as he ended the call. Now his 2013 Black Lexus left the Washington, DC city border and he continued on to Bethesda, Maryland. Meanwhile all Frank Carter could think about was the possibility that he may have the biggest scoop in modern history and yet he did not know the full extent of it for that matter. It was one that may not only affect the course of American history, but the history of the world at the same time as well.

Delta Airlines flight 863 was on its final leg from its starting point at Los Angeles. As the flight crew began to prepare for its landing in Chicago, they continued their conversation about the Chicago Bears upsetting the Green Bay Packers a day earlier.

"I think Green Bay had that game!" the pilot began as he added "There was no way that tackle by the Bears linesman was clean!"

"I beg to differ!" shot back the co-pilot "That tackle was as clean as any out there."

"It was unnecessary roughness! I saw that play over and over again." the pilot argued.

"Only a Packers fan would say that." the flight engineer mused.

"We lost our quarterback for the rest of the season at least if not permanently!" the pilot noted "We were on the brink of going to the Super Bowl and winning it."

"It's only November 23 and you have Green Bay going all the way." the co-pilot argued "I don't think so!"

"And you think your Bears will win it all?" the pilot wondered aloud with a smirk.

"We weren't implying that!" the flight engineer protested.

"You could have fooled me." the pilot snarled.

"Why so serious? It's only a game." the co-pilot noted.

"Only a game?" the pilot thought aloud as he reached into his pocket and whipped out a box cutter quickly slitting the throats of his co-pilot as well as his flight engineer. The pilot then locked the cockpit door and then began to complete his plans for where he actually intended Flight 863 to land.

One of the security guards watching the monitors at the Galleria Mall was beginning to lose his focus. He was observing nothing unusual. Meanwhile Carl came in and they were discussing the day's events among themselves. For the most part there was nothing out of the ordinary going on with the exception of a few shoplifters.

"Other than that, nothing has occurred." Carl surmised in reference to the shoplifters.

"That is correct." the guard replied.

"I was sent in to relieve you." Carl replied. The guard now left to have his lunch in the food court. Carl then looked around and began to tinker with some of the equipment. The security camera system quickly crashed. Carl then left the room and made his way to the TGI Friday restaurant and bar that was inside the Galleria for some lunch himself.

"They are having trouble taking us seriously." Ian Daley began as he talked to both Agents Bishop and Townsend on speakerphone. "It seems that our message is being ignored every step of the way."

"If I didn't know any better I would say that there are some people here who may be involved." Agent Bishop replied.

"Nothing would surprise me given how today has been going so far." Agent Townsend noted.

"I'm with you." Ian Daley concurred.

"This is an outrage when Homeland Security which was created for the purpose of preventing a terrorist attack from occurring is actually creating the conditions in which a terrorist attack will occur." Agent Downey acknowledged.

"As American citizens this is something that we should be terrified about and rightfully so." Agent Norman began as he then added "I thought that we learned our lessons about what led up to 9/11. After all these years we all have been mistaken after all and tragically so I might add."

"At least we are doing something that the rest of these boneheads are doing." Daley began "That is to prevent a terrorist attack from occurring. Although there are only five of us, we are going to continue to fight this uphill battle until we are no longer able to fight it."

"I have an idea." Agent Bishop began.

"Do share this idea with us." Ian Daley inquired.

"I know Frank Carter from *The Washington Post*." Agent Bishop began "I have no question that he will definitely help us spread the word. That alone may increase our chances of preventing an attack from occurring."

"I say we do it." Agent Townsend started "What do we have to lose by alerting Frank Carter about this imminent threat."

"I'm going to place that call." Ian Daley responded as he placed the call to Frank Carter. Carter quickly picked up his cellphone while he was at lunch and said "Frank Carter. How may I help you?"

"Frank." Ian began "It's me Ian Daley from Homeland Security."

"Ian, how can I help you?" Frank Carter inquired.

"Frank I need you to listen very carefully to what I am about to say." Ian began.

"I'm all ears Ian." Carter replied.

"Frank I have reason to believe that the shooting of Eric Watson was the signal to give al-Qaeda the go ahead to carry out a terrorist attack that may be very imminent. This is just like when the Taliban assassinated Massoud just two days before the September 11th attacks took place. Homeland Security has not taken this threat seriously. We have been alerting the malls about this and they are acting like that this is a crank call. Frank, I need you to get the word out about this."

"Just how certain are you that this threat may be carried out?" Carter asked.

"I'm very certain but I cannot prove it one hundred percent though. The signals indicate that it is likely that the malls may be among the targets of a terrorist attack." Daley continued.

"I am going to go on Twitter as well as Facebook and get the word out." Carter noted as the clock was now minutes away from two o'clock.

"Tim." began Paul Samson "I understand that you have been placing a series of calls to the other managers of SPG to inform them of a possible terrorist threat at my malls. Could you elaborate on this?"

"Paul." Tim Lake began "I have a long time friend who works in Homeland Security. He is very certain that the malls may be among the targets of such an attack. I am not one hundred percent certain about this, but I highly recommend that we are on the highest alert possible just in case."

"Tim are you aware of the resources this would require." Samson mused aloud.

"Paul, are you aware of the tragedy and damages that would occur from such an attack?" Tim Lake began as he quickly added "Do I have to remind you of the lawsuits that would be filed against us because we failed to prevent an attack from occurring despite the fact that we have prior knowledge beforehand."

"Are you asking me for the green light to go ahead with these precautions?" Paul asked.

"No, I am informing you that I have alerted the other mall managers of this potential threat while I have been taking precautions to make sure that such an attack does not occur." Lake responded.

"So you are going ahead with these preparations without my approval." Paul Samson mused.

"Considering the fact that you did not reply to my many messages regarding this very important matter of the highest order, I had no choice but to go ahead and conduct the process of protecting the Galleria Mall from a terrorist attack. I never thought that in my lifetime that such a threat would be facing us. Now I have no question that this threat is on the brink of occurring. It is my job to make sure that it does not occur."

"Tim, you have a blank check from me to do whatever you need to do to prevent a Westgate Mall or even a Mumbai style terrorist attack from occurring." Paul Samson ordered Tim Lake. After Samson was done, he sent out a text regarding this potential threat while giving the other mall managers of the Samson Property Group a blank check to do whatever it takes to prevent a terrorist attack from occurring.

The time was now one fifty three pm Eastern as the time in Riyadh, Saudi Arabia was ten fifty three pm and in Kabul, Afghanistan the time was eleven twenty three pm. Jabril Alawi immediately logged onto the eTrade website. He saw the status of his account. He was pleased with how he was doing with his investments. Now the then clicked on the transaction icon and it then asked him whether he wanted to buy or sell shares of stock. He clicked on sell and the list of his investments showed up on the screen. Alawi scrolled down to Cypress and clicked on the Cypress name. The screen then asked him how many shares he would like to sell. Jabril typed in all of his shares in Cypress and clicked the sell icon. Within seconds the shares of Cypress were sold. Alawi then went back to the main page of the transactions and clicked on the buy icon. He typed in Pan Arabian Oil and the screen asked him how many shares he would like to buy. Jabril the price for one share of Pan Arabian Oil stock and he quickly decided to buy five hundred thousand shares. The transaction would take a moment before it was completed.

Meanwhile Hans Gubioso was typing away at his laptop inside his palatial mansion in Zurich, Switzerland. He then noticed a massive dumping of shares of Cypress, Incorporated as well as the sudden spike in the purchase of Pan Arabian Oil at the same time. Hans then took a glance and he realized that he had conducted two other transactions of that nature. He quickly came to a conclusion that it was some sort of signal. The extent of the signal would soon be known globally. Hans then placed a call to the Securities and Exchange Commission in New York City and received a recorded introduction. As each question was asked through a computer recorded voice, Gubioso pressed a number that would correspond with the appropriate question. Now the computer recorded voice then said "Please wait for the next available representative to take your call." Hans now rolled his eyes in disgust knowing that he may not be able to get his warning in on time.

2:00pm

"Look at the clear blue skies." Scott Shepherd said to his four year old son Scottie.

"I see it! I see it!" Scottie replied "I see sky!"

"What color is the sky?" Scott asked.

"It's boo, it's boo." Scottie responded.

"It's blue not boo. Can you say blue?" Scott inquired.

"Boo! Blue!" Scottie said as he now saw a plane flying near the Sears Tower. "Look Daddy! Plane! Plane!"

"I see the plane." Scott replied as it now flew towards the Sears Tower. He now put his hands over his son's eyes and said "We are going to play peekaboo." Knowing there could be an aviation mishap at any moment. He began to run with his son. As they ran away from the Sears Tower, they heard a very loud crash and then a series of explosions just seconds later.

"Hello." said a representative from the Securities and Exchange Commission "How can I help you."

"I'm Hans Gubioso from Zurich, Switzerland "There has been a spike in the sale of Cypress Stock as well the sudden increase in the purchase of Pan Arabian Oil all by the same individuals. These transactions have raised a red flag."

"What do you want us to do about it?" the representative asked.

"That's why I called you to begin with. I would like a little guidance about what to do about this if that is not going to take up too much of your time." Hans shot back.

"What do you think could occur as a result of these series of transactions?" the rep then inquired.

"A terrorist attack of course." Gubioso stated.

"Just how does a series of sales in stock result in a terrorist attack?" the rep then mused.

"These transactions have been conducted by people who are from the Middle East for crying out loud! Are you Americans that dense?" Gubioso exploded as the representative said "How dare you talk to me that way!"

"No, how dare you dismiss this potential terrorist threat and not take it seriously!" Gubioso shot back "All I wanted to do was get the word out about a terrorist threat and alert you idiots as well as Homeland Security and this is the thanks I get around here!"

"Look we have never dealt with a call of this magnitude!' the representative exploded "We don't know how exactly to handle it as she then said "I need to bring my supervisor over so we can discuss how to reroute your call. Homeland Security must be alerted about this at once." A supervisor then came over and she said "I am on the line with an investment banker from Zurich, Switzerland. He is concerned that a series of similar transactions by a group of traders in the Middle East may signal a terrorist attack may be impending."

"I would like to speak to him." He began while adding "Please call this number." Which he scribbled on a piece of paper "This will get you to a representative from the Department of Homeland Security. Stay on the line until you begin to speak to a representative. Once you are done informing the representative about what you were just told, hand the phone to me and I will handle it from there." As a loud explosion quickly tore through the office which ended not only the conversation, but the lives of countless millions of New York City residents at the same time.

"What on earth just happened?!" Hans Gubioso panicked as the line suddenly went dead during the explosion that was so loud it not only sent a series of excruciatingly sharp pain throughout his left ear, but off threw off his balance at the same time. As Gubioso began to regain his composure he immediately realized the full extent of what happened. Hans quickly placed a call to the management department of his brokerage company and said "I need to speak to whoever is in charge of freezing accounts."

"Can you tell me what is going on?' the representative inquired.

"I am concerned that a series of transactions may have been a signal for a terrorist attack which may have just taken place." Gubioso said.

"Can you please give me the specifics of the transactions?" he then asked.

"It seems that a group of traders from the Middle East sold all of their shares of Cypress, Incorporated and bought Pan Arabian Oil in its place." Hans noted.

"We will place a call to the Securities Department of the Swiss government immediately in order to figure out how to proceed with this matter." the representative said as he then made the phone call. An operator picked up the phone and asked "How can I help you?"

"We have a situation in which a group of Middle Eastern men have been suddenly selling Cypress, incorporated stock and buying Pan Arabian oil. Given the explosion that one of my traders heard on the other end of the phone while alerting the Securities and Exchange Commission in New York City about these series of transactions. There is a concern that the sales were a precursor for an impending terrorist attack to take place if one has not occurred as of yet."

"I will have my supervisor handle the call." the representative replied as he then alerted the supervisor who then handled the call. Once the supervisor for the Securities Department of the Swiss Government was motioned over. He was then informed about the unfolding situation. "I must speak with him at once." As he then spoke to representative of the Swiss brokerage firm who placed the call. "What is going on?' he inquired.

"We may have a situation on our hands in which a group of Middle Eastern men have been selling Cypress, Incorporated stock and buying Pan Arabian Oil stock in its place. This has been occurring throughout the day and has proliferated exponentially within the past twenty minutes." he began as the official cut him off by saying "The BBC is now reporting terrorist attacks have taken place in New York and Chicago within the past ten minutes." he gasped while adding "I am alerting the president about how to take care of this situation." The two now talked for what seemed to be minutes. The official then placed one call to the Securities and Exchange Commission while he motioned another supervisor over and that person placed a call to the Department of Homeland Security.

"Oh great, the line is dead!' the official snarled as he then placed a call to Washington, DC and he would have to endure endless computer recorded messages while waiting to warn an operator about an impending terrorist attack which may take place during the wait in order to speak to someone about a preventing a terrorist attack from taking place.

"Mr. President." Pat Ryan began "A 747 has just crashed into the Sears Tower."

"A 747 has just crashed into the Los Alamos power plant." Chet Jackson added as he raced into the room and turned on CNN "Here is the footage of a 747 that has just crashed into the Empire State Building."

"New York, Chicago, Los Alamos . . ." President Wolcott began as the phone began to ring on his desk "I just heard about New York, Chicago and Los Alamos."

"Our fleet in the Persian Gulf has just been crippled." Secretary of Defense Alan Rhodes replied as he then saw form outside his window three more 747's heading in their direction "We must go to our bunkers . . ." as the planes crashed into their intended targets and the conversation on both ends of the phone came to a sudden and permanent stop. The White House, the Pentagon as well as the Capital Building where both houses had been debating about the election became vaporized. This was a result of the suitcase nukes that were brought aboard the planes.

"What just happened?" the official from the Swiss government bellowed as the call was suddenly cut off as a result of the nuclear strike on Washington, DC. Now the BBC network interrupted its breaking news coverage of the attacks in both New York City and Chicago. "We have just received reports of a nuclear strike on Washington, DC just a moment ago."

"That figures!" he exploded while he then tried to alert the Swiss leader about the attacks. He was now concerned that there may no longer be a United States of America in existence by the time the Swiss leader was put on the line.

"How soon until you two will be coming home?" Ian Daley asked Irene.

"As soon as we finished the last round of shopping for the day and I would say we should be done in an hour." Irene replied.

"You two need to come home now!" Ian began "Hijacked planes have crashed into the Sears Tower, the Empire State

Building, the Space needle, the Los Alamos and Indian Point power plants . . . Oh God No!"

"What is it Dad?" Irene asked with a panicked tone in her voice.

"Three more planes have crashed into the White House, the Pentagon and the Capital Building!" Ian gasped "Get out of the mall now!" he ordered his twin daughters.

"Irene!" Irma panicked as the two now heard noises from what seemed to be a machine gun while herds of people were racing in their direction. As the twins were eating their lunch in the food court of the Galleria they quickly cut their lunch short in order to race out. Now Saleh Bowadi stood in the center of the food court and bellowed "Allahu Akbar!" began to fire away at everyone. He quickly reached inside his suicide vest and pressed the button blowing himself up killing scores of people in the process.

"Agent Bishop." began their charge "I need you and Agent Downey to get back ASAP! The White House, the Pentagon and the U.S, Capital Building has been attacked!"

"We're on our way." Bishop replied as he turned to Agent Downey and said "We need to head back to FBI headquarters at once! Washington's been attacked. They took out the white House, the Pentagon and the Capital Building!"

"That Daley guy was right after all!" Downey panicked as they hopped into Bishop's FBI issued car and left the parking lot of CIA headquarters. They began to speed down the main road and quickly heard a series of loud explosions. "What on earth was that?" Downey bellowed as he looked through the rear view window and saw the explosion at CIA headquarters "Those punks just took out Langley!" in reference to CIA headquarters.

"This has to be some kind of an inside job!" Agent Bishop exploded "No one can take down Langley without being detected beforehand!" as he called the J. Edgar Hoover Building.

"Hello?"

"Langley was just attacked!" Agent Bishop panicked.

"I've changed my mind. Don't return here. Go to the nearest safe house and stay . . ." he began as a voice on his intercom system said "A van is pulling up to the front entrance and . . ." as an explosion was heard in the background ending the phone call between Agent Bishop and his boss.

"What happened?" Agent Downey replied as Agent Bishop quickly accelerated the speed of his car.

"It looks like FBI Headquarters has been attacked as well!" Agent Bishop bellowed "We're going to the nearest safe house and hunkering down!"

"My brother, the operation is proceeding as planned." Khalid Isawi said to Jabril Alawi as they were cryptically discussing the terrorist attack in the United States.

"Praise Allah that the infidels are finally getting what they have long deserved." Alawi replied as they were watching the coverage of the terrorist attacks on the live feed from the al-Jazeera website. The news of the operation being a success was the best news that they have ever heard. They were beginning to realize that the best news was yet to come on this very day when they received word about the nuclear strike "Allahu Akbar!" he then noted knowing that the day can only get better from there."

"This time I don't think that the infidels will attack us like they did after the September 11th Attacks!" Isawi observed "We have definitely crippled them this time around! We can now concentrate of focusing our energies on liberating Palestine and taking it back for our people!"

"With the Americans out of the picture we can now concentrate all of our efforts as well as all of our energies on taking down Great Britain while liberating Palestine and driving the Zionist infidel occupiers into the Mediterranean Sea once and for all." Alawi noted.

"We have taken down our biggest threat to our cause to date. Now the rest should be very easy for us." Isawi started "We have enough of our brothers in Great Britain in order to coordinate our efforts there."

"How soon until we begin our operation there?" Alawi inquired.

"Watch al-Jazeera. Trust me." Isawi noted.

"Are they beginning to leave yet?" Mohammad Aziz asked Salim Ubadi as Ubadi was keeping watch over the rear exit of the parliament building in London while Aziz was watching the main from entrance of the Parliament building.

"Nothing yet." Ubadi began "They're still debating over Prime Minister Halston's no confidence vote." as he was listening to the parliamentary debate on the British Broadcasting Channel. Now Aziz received a text on his phone. He then said "Excuse me." as he looked at the text with the message "Now!" he then said to Aziz "It's time!" With that the two men placed their rocket launchers in the windows their respective apartments and quickly fired them as the all-out attack on the parliament building began. Soon as the first two missiles stuck the building, it was the cue for the other attackers to detonate the truck bombs which were strategically placed outside the Parliament building. The British Prime Minister and the entire Parliament would suffer brutally painful, but quick deaths at the same time.

"We are now receiving unconfirmed reports of simultaneous terrorist attacks in both the United States as well as London." the BBC announcer began as he broke the news of the terrorist attacks "The Parliament building has been reportedly attacked by rocket launchers." he continued as the patrons of an upscale restaurant began to request their checks so they could pay for their order and quickly leave.

"We need to get out and fast. They attacked the White House, the Capital Building as well as the Pentagon not to mention various malls and other cities throughout the United States." Clive Daley began as he began to place a phone call to his American cousin Ian Daley. Clive Daley was of medium height and build just like his younger cousin by a year. Clive's hair had a touch of gray unlike Ian. The MI-5 agent was now becoming concerned that this could be an all-out attack and that there was the possibility that Israel could be next. Now Clive heard a voice in the direction of the center of the restaurant bellow "Allahu Akbar!" Just before Clive could take his 357 Magnum out of his pocket, the suicide bomber detonated himself killed many in his wake. Similar scenes were now playing out throughout London as well as throughout Great Britain. At the same time, Moslem soldiers in the military of Great Britain began to open fire on their native British national counterparts as an all-out Islamic revolt began to take place in Great Britain while suicide bombers began to detonate themselves with dirty bombs in all of the English cities.

Israeli Defense Minister Eli Shlivi was partaking in his evening ritual of reading his Torah. He was in the middle of chapter eight of the book of Exodus. The story of Moses putting curses on Pharaoh as well as the Egyptians on order to let the Israelites who they enslaved could go out and pray to Yahweh was now in its second night. As the fifty three year old whose family had lived in the Holy Land for at least seven centuries was halfway through chapter eight, his cellphone rang. Shlivi answered the phone. "Hello."

"You need to go on Skype for an emergency cabinet meeting immediately." said the person who made the call to the Israeli Defense Minister. It was Prime Minister Elihu on the other line. He quickly hung up the phone. Shlivi immediately called the person who was on his call list should an emergency meeting of the Israeli cabinet ever take place via Skype. He called Transportation Minister Herzog and said "The Prime Minister has called for an emergency cabinet meeting on Skype to take place immediately." The cabinet ministers quickly logged onto their Skype accounts and then Israeli Prime Minister Herschel Elihu addressed everyone who was present for the meeting

"Just moments ago an all-out terrorist attack has taken place throughout both the United States as well as Great Britain." Prime Minister Elihu began as he was in the process of addressing his cabinet "Numerous cities throughout the two nations have been attacked while the Mossad has now informed me that the governments of both the United States as well as Great Britain have been decapitated. I am ordering that Israeli is to immediately be put on the highest alert possible both domestically as well as our foreign interests. I am ordering the Israeli military and police to round up every Palestinian as well as every Israeli Arab for detention until further notice. The threat for Israeli to be attack is at its highest level possible. It could occur any second now. This is why I say that timing is of the essence. We cannot afford to go through another Holocaust just like our families endured during World War II. The militaries of both the United States as well as Great Britain have also been crippled as a result of the attacks. The concern here is how soon until we are the next nation to be attacked."

"I am in the process of putting our military on full alert!" Israeli Defense Minister Shlivi began as he had just found out about the simultaneous terrorist attacks throughout the United States as well as Great Britain. "I have no question that we will be the next nation that is to be attacked!"

"In that case put everyone on alert and get the troops ready to engage in battle." Prime Minister Elihu replied while the other ministers concurred during an emergency Skype conference call at the homes of each cabinet minister given the gravity of the attacks that took place overseas "I am also ordering every minister not to leave their homes until further notice since the governments of the United States as well as Great Britain have been both decapitated."

Meanwhile the sirens began to blare throughout Israel. This was the signal for every Israeli who was of military age as well as those who have served previously or presently are serving in the Israeli military. As every active, retired as well as reserve member of the military got into their vehicles and began to make their way to the nearest military base in which they were assigned to, all they could think of was the extreme gravity of the situation that they were presently facing at this very moment in time in the history of Israel. The horror of facing potentially ahnillation for the second time within the past one hundred years rallied every member of the Jewish race both in Israel as well as overseas to engage in battle. Those who born after the Holocaust took place never forgot the stories that their families, friends, teachers as well as rabbis shared with them about the worst atrocities in which any race could ever face. The horror of a race of people to be ahniliated once was beyond horrific to bear, but twice within the span of a century further insensed the Jewish race. This was their time to defend their people once and for all.

"I think they are coming now." a young Palestinian male in his early twenties said to his comrade. They were beginning to aim their submachine guns at the caravan of cars who were heading to the Israeli military bases in order to ready themselves to engage in battle for the nation of Israel. As the first wave of cars was now passing by them, they took out their hand grenades and hurled it at each car which was driving along the road. As the grenades began to detonate, they took out their machine guns and began to spray the members of the Israeli military with bullets. "Allahu Akbar!" they cried "The liberation of Palestine has begun!" Similar scenes were beginning to play out all across Israel. Meanwhile those who were on their way to their nearest military base took out their weapons and began to engage in battle with the Palestinians albeit somewhat unsuccessfully in the beginning.

"Allahu Akbar!" screamed another Palestinian terrorist as he pressed the detonator button of his suicide vest and detonated the dirty bomb in Tel Aviv as similar scenes also began to play out all over Israel. Meanwhile Jerusalem was the only city that was not detonated with a dirty bomb. Instead the Palestinians were mowing down the Israelis with their weapons while trying to liberate the Holy City from the Zionists.

2:45pm

"We can now confirm that at least twenty four passenger planes have crashed into the Sears Tower, The Empire State Building, the Pentagon, the White House, the U.S. Congress, the CIA and FBI headquarters, targets in Las Vegas, Los Angeles, Boston, and Miami as well as nuclear power plants, ports and airports. Trucks have exploded in front of local FBI as well as federal buildings while security units were mobilizing to be deployed. We are also receiving reports where across the nation, shopping malls are being massacred, and the main hubs of the national media have been attacked. There has been an all-out cyber-attack as well. We are now receiving reports that twelve U.S. task forces, the main military instillations as well as bases are being attacked." the local news reporter from outside Bethesda, Maryland noted "This unprecedented act of terrorism coming during a presidential recount that may further divide America. The Presidential and Vice Presidential candidates for both parties we can now confirm have been assassinated in the attacks. What we must ask ourselves is who is left to lead the United States as anarchy is just starting throughout the nation. Just how do we combat an enemy where we do not have a military nor do we have a governmental chain of command present?"

"We should have been much better prepared for this." Ian Daley began as he was speaking to FBI Agent Rob Bishop on his cellphone "I kept warning those morons at Homeland Security that the malls were going to be attacked as well as other targets. Now to attack other nations at the same time . . ." he added as he heard the NPR coverage of the attacks.

"Did you see the other targets coming?" Agent Bishop inquired as he cut off Ian Daley.

"I saw some of them, but as usual my comments fell on deaf ears." Daley replied with rage in his voice "What else is new with them."

"Ian, the clowns at Homeland Security were killed in the attacks. You did all you could do. We need you to help us get those who attacked us." Bishop stated.

"Whatever you need me to do I will do!" Ian replied emphatically.

"We are now receiving unconfirmed reports of dirty bombs as well as suicide bombers attacking several U.S. cities. New York, Boston, Philadelphia, Washington, Charlotte, Atlanta, Miami, Orlando, New Orleans, Nashville, Indianapolis, Chicago, Minneapolis, St. Paul, Kansas City, St. Louis, Las Vegas, Dallas, Houston, Oklahoma City, Denver, Phoenix, Los Angeles, San Francisco, San Diego, Sacramento, Portland and Seattle are among those cities that have been attacked." the local news reporter from outside Bethesda, Maryland continued as he then paused and quickly added "There are unconfirmed reports of simultaneous attacks taking place in both Great Britain as well as Israel at this hour. From all indications the parliament building, Buckingham Palace, and numerous cafes, pubs as well as concert halls have been attacked in Great Britain while dirty bombs have been detonated in London, Wimbledon, Glasgow, and Manchester as well as other cities. From all accounts, the British government as well as the British monarchy has been for all practical purposes decapitated in the attacks. In Israel, massacres are taking place in which convoys of members of the Israeli Military and their reservists are engaging in an all-out fire fight at this hour. Palestinian gunmen have opened fire on the soldiers as they were heading to their military bases in order to receive their battle instructions. Meanwhile Jerusalem has become a war zone with Palestinian terrorists attacking the Jewish and Christian residents in the Holy City in an effort to liberate it in the name of Islam. Also, dirty bombs have been detonated in Tel Aviv, Haifa, as well as several other cities and villages throughout Israel. There are strong indications that this is an all-out attack that is being orchestrated by al-Qaeda, Hamas as well as quite possibly Hezbollah."

"This just keeps getting worse and worse by the second!" Ian Daley gasped.

"We need to get started now." Agent Bishop began "Meet me and Agent Downey outside the Galleria ASAP."

"I'm on my way." Daley said as he raced out of his house and began to make his way to the Galleria.

"There you have it." Ayman al-Zawahiri began as his face was swelling with pride over the destruction he had just inflicted on the infidels "The best news is yet to come."

"What could be better than this?" Khalid Isawi inquired. He was the number two man in al-Qaeda "The destruction of the Jews and the liberation of Palestine?"

"That is in the process of happening right now but that is not what I was inferring to." al-Zawahiri noted.

"Then what were you inferring to?" Isawi then asked.

"You will find out soon enough. It will happen before their day is finished." he said as they were now watching the latest news on their strike on Al-Jazeera.

Frank Carter was now stuck in a traffic jam. He was on his way to meet with Agent Bishop when he heard the news of the attacks. Carter then received a phone call from Agent Bishop and he quickly answered the phone "Agent Bishop, I hope you and Agent Downey are both safe."

"Yes we're safe. I hope that you're alright as well." Agent Bishop inquired.

"Yes. I was able to leave Washington before the attacks." Carter said "The president won't be conducting that investigation after all." he added in reference to the president's death.

"Vice President Thomas, Governor Freeman and his running mate Senator Tomkins were also killed." Agent Bishop noted.

"What have we come to as a nation?" Carter mused "The Democrats tamper with the votes in order to make the Republicans look bad, the government has been decapitated in a terrorist attack as well as our military and most of the nation and our national security apparatus has completely failed us. We took all these precautions in order to prevent another September 11th from taking place and we have an attack that is a thousand times worse! This is a complete and utter failure!"

"I don't even know who is next in line to become president after what happened?" Bishop wondered aloud.

"I'm wondering myself." Carter added as he then asked "Where are you?"

"We're almost at the Galleria. Come and join us there." Bishop offered Carter.

"I will be there as soon as possible given all of the traffic." Carter noted.

"We are now receiving reports that House Speaker Nathan Grumbly has survived the attacks. The Speaker of the House was not in Washington when the attacks took place almost an hour ago. He will be sworn in momentarily as our next president." the National Public Radio reporter announced.

"This day has just got even worse!" Ian Daley yelled as he was now pulling his car into a nearby parking lot. He leaped out of his car and raced over to the mall where Agents Bishop and Downey were waiting for him. "Is there any news on Irene and Irma?" as he began to bolt his way through the yellow tape.

"Ian we don't know yet." Agent Bishop replied as he and Agent Downey both began to restrain him "Please don't go in there! The mall is well secured."

"But my girls are in there!" Daley screamed.

"The police are handling it. We need you to help us with another aspect of the investigation." Agent Bishop said as he and Agent Downey were able to restrain him and bring him to a secluded area. "What happened at the Homeland Security this morning? Why are you not there right now?"

"I was sent home by Reggie Patterson. I got into an argument with both him and Hervey Harrison over securing the malls in order to prevent a terrorist attack. "Both Patterson and Harrison did not think it was a good idea though."

"And look what happened because of their incompetence." Bishop stated.

"As they always say nothing changes when it comes to bureaucracy." Agent Downey noted as he rolled his eyes "I thought we learned our lesson after September 11th. We definitely assumed wrong on that one."

"Ian, there is something I think you need to know." Agent Bishop began "Harrison and Patterson as well as the rest of the members of Homeland Security who were present when the attack took place were killed. How people were not working when the attack took place?"

"I'm not sure. I was sent home around three this morning. I am unable to help you there." Daley replied.

"For all practical purposes you are the new Director of Homeland Security." Bishop said as Daley then went limp. He was now the head of a cabinet level position. Ian Walter Daley was now responsible for the prevention of future terrorist attacks against the United States of America.

"Nathan Grumbly was not in Washington at the time of the attacks. He is about to be sworn in as our next president." a reporter for WBMD said as he was now breaking the news.

"What?" Agent Bishop quickly snapped.

"Speaker Grumbly was not in the nation's capital when it was attacked." Daley repeated.

"Can you hold that thought for a little while?" Agent Bishop said to Agent Downey knowing just what he was going to say "Agent Downey and I need to make a phone call. Can you come with us? I think we may have you speak to someone." The three then went to the main roadway and began to walk down the street until they found a payphone. Bishop then placed a call to Frank Carter, but the line was dead. "What is going on?" Agent Bishop asked as he was now feeling very panicked "I just spoke to him a few moments ago."

"The cellular technology is down." Daley responded. The three now began to return to the secluded area when they heard a beep from a car horn. They quickly jumped and then saw Frank Carter sitting in his car during a traffic jam. Carter rolled down the window and said "Hop on in." The three men got into Carter's new black Lexus that has just came off the assembly line for all practical purposes.

"I see that you brought along Ian Daley for the ride." Frank remarked.

"That would be correct sir." Bishop replied.

"How are you and the twins holding up Ian?" Carter then asked. He and Daley have gone back a lot of years and have maintained a great friendship since they first arrived in Washington, DC during the mid-1980's.

"Not good." Daley began "The twins were in the Galleria when the attack took place."

"A little bird told me that you had a little falling out with Homeland Security late last night and they sent you home." Carter began as he then added "Some gratitude they showed you. All you did was try to warn them where the attack would take place and they unceremoniously threw you out. What is the matter with our governmental agencies? Their employees try to do the right thing and it is never appreciated. I thought they had learned their lesson from September 11th."

"I'm afraid that it has become a common theme today." Agent Bishop acknowledged.

"Yes." Agent Bishop and Ian Daley replied almost in unison.

"Sir." Agent Bishop began "Ian has something to tell you."

"Speaker Grumbly may have survived the attack. He was not in Washington when the attacks took place." Daley replied.

"Hold up!" Carter then said "Our esteemed speaker of the house was not present when the attacks took place?" he now sputtered.

"That would be correct." Daley noted.

"If this is then we could be looking at something completely different." Carter added.

"Would you care to tell me how different?" Daley then asked.

"I need some time to comprehend this." Carter started "Once I am able to digest everything, I will let the three of you know exactly what I am thinking.

"We have crippled them!" Ishmael Younis proclaimed to Khalid Isawi over the phone "There is no way that the infidels will be able to fight back now! This is the greatest moment in the history of Islam to date! Praise be to Allah! Today the Americans, the British as well the Jews! We will smote our enemies from existence!"

"Imagine the joy that our people must feel!" Isawi began while continuing on "The notion of an Islamic Caliphate extending to all of the corners of the Earth is beyond joy for us to comprehend! Allahu Akbar!"

"Allah is definitely smiling down upon us on this very sacred day. He has begun to carry out his judgment against the infidels once and for all!" Ishmael beamed "Imagine the numbers of brothers who are entering paradise at this very moment! They are only beginning to experience the land flowing with milk and honey as well as the seventy two virgins at the disposal of each of our heroes! What a joyous day for Islam!" as they began to watch the first photos of the United States after the destruction that they just had helped to unleash only fifty minutes earlier. The aerial cameras were showing the ruins of the cities in which, New York, Chicago as well as Las Vegas had previously stood. Crumbled buildings as well as vaporized marks where buildings previously stood could be seen from the skies. Also another camera zoomed in on New York City and showed shadows made of vapor where people were standing when the attacks took place. Another camera began to show the carnage from inside the Galleria mall that showed shattered glass, debris as well as blood throughout the mall. Another camera began to show mobs of people beginning to loot stores in small towns as well as cites in the United States there were not attacked by al-Qaeda within the past hour. "Those infidels or I should say whatever is left of them are running around like they are chickens with their heads cut off. They no longer have any leadership alive for that matter!"

"Right now those Zionists who have annexed Palestine and driving our brothers out are experiencing the same thing. Soon they will know how we felt when they drove out not only of our homes, but out of our land of Palestine as well" Isawi gushed.

"Our great leader did not revealed to us when he would carry out the Palestine Operation." Younis said in reference to Ayman al-Zawahiri. "The pride that we all feel right now as Moslems is beyond immeasurable." he added as they continued to watch the coverage of what is known to them as Operation Yarmuk while the rest of the world is referring to it as November 23 or 11/23.

"Hans." began the supervisor of his Swiss investment banking firm "You have a phone call from an FBI agent from America he continued in reference to Agent Townsend while he handed his cellphone to Gubioso.

"Hello." Hans said.

"Hans Gubioso?" Agent Bishop asked making sure that he was speaking to Hans Gubioso.

"Yes, I'm Hans Gubioso." he replied "How may I help you?"

"I am Agent Bishop from the Federal Bureau of Investigation in the United States. I just received a tip from the Mossad in Israel that you may have a lead for us regarding the attacks."

"Yes." Gubioso replied as he then continued "I have a number of very wealthy clients who are either based in the Middle East or who either presently reside there or are of Arab descent. They simultaneously sold all of their shares of Cypress, incorporated stock that they had bought over the summer and bought Pan Arabian Oil stock at the same time."

"Why do you think that these transactions may be connected to the attack?" Agent Bishop inquired while already knowing the answer but also trying to prove his point in the process that the shooting of the Ohio Secretary of State Eric

Harris was a signal for not only the terrorist attacks but the mass transactions of Cypress and Pan Arabian Oil.

"The reason why I feel that is way is that it was not only the timing of the sale, but the company that they replaced Cypress, incorporated in their investment portfolios with. The idea of replacing a company that may be responsible for the voting scandal in the United States with one that may increase exponentially due to what could become an unprecedented spike in the price of oil brings about great alarm for me. I had to get the warning out. I wish that there was more time to prevent this from happening." Hans replied with great sorrow in his voice.

"You did more than what our intelligence agency have done combined overall in trying to prevent this from taking place." Agent Bishop noted.

"I did sense that I had to yell at a member of your Securities and Exchange Commission just to convince them that this was not a joke. They were being very dismissive of this until I let them have it between the eyes figuratively that is." Gubioso noted.

"Just so you know." Agent Bishop began "Yelling at most of the employees at the governmental agencies in the United States does not wake them up as to what is going on. I thought you should know that. By the way, I would like to learn the secret about how to even get them to wake up at a future date." he suggested.

"Just how do you deal with the incompetence that is running rampant throughout your nation? It has resulted in not one, but as of now two terrorist attacks because of it." Hans wondered aloud.

"We are a nation who as a whole does not learn from its past mistakes." Agent Bishop noted.

"I can tell." Gubioso acknowledged. "Anyways, when I was able to speak to someone who could be able to give me the proper guidance about how to report my concern, the attack took place."

"I am going to relay this to my team." Agent Bishop began "If I have any more questions, I will get back to you as soon as the questions arise. Thank you for your help."

"I just wish that the calls came sooner and this whole thing could have been averted in the process." Hans added as the conversation came to an end.

The battles throughout Israeli continued to rage on. Every Israeli citizen raced out of their homes with weapons and began to fight the Palestinians. Meanwhile, the Palestinians raced out for their homes and began to fight the Israelis. Meanwhile in the West Bank as well as the Gaza Strip, the Palestinians found out about the attack on the radio.

"The Americans, British and Zionists have been attacked!" a Palestinian male in his early twenties beamed with pride "The American and British governments as well as their nations are no longer in existence! The liberation of Palestine has begun!" The news spread very quickly as each Palestinian gathered their weapons out and began to leave their respective villages as an army. They would quickly merge with other marching bands of Palestinians to form one massive army. Soon many Arabs especially those who lived in Egypt, Lebanon, Syria, Jordan and Iraq as well as Iran also began to join in on the battle wither it would be by car or by plane. A ferry boat of Saudi Arabian citizens also began to make the trek across the Red Sea in order to help their Palestinian brethren fight the Zionist occupiers. Soon all would converge upon the Israelis and Palestinians who have already been fighting not only on the streets throughout Israel, but in Jerusalem as well.

"Are they ready?" the Iranian president inquired of his secretary of the military in reference to the nuclear warheads. He had been watching live coverage of the attacks on the United States, Great Britain as well as Israel.

"Yes." he replied "We are awaiting your order to destroy the Jewish State once and for all. Is this a great day for our people or what. It is even better that it has occurred on our hold day of the week!" he said while swelling with pride.

"The Zionist threat will soon cease to exist." The Iranian president noted as he now said "I will alert the leaders of Iraq, Lebanon, Syria and Jordan to commence Operation Palestine." As he now called the leaders of the four Arab nations so they could begin their strike against Israel which they still call Palestine to this day as well.

3:00pm

"Speaker Grumbly repeat after me." The 16th Court of Appeals Justice Judge Oliver Plank began "I, Nathan Aaron Grumbly do solemnly swear." Plank began. Judge Plank was of smallish build and portly. His flowing black robe covered his brown suit, white shirt and tan tie. He was balding with no hair left on the top of his head. He had white hair, a mustache and a beard as well. His steel gray eyes pierced through the room.

"I, Nathan Aaron Grumbly do solemnly swear." Grumbly replied.

"That I will faithfully execute the office of President of the United States." Plank continued.

"That I will faithfully execute the office of President of the United States." Grumbly repeated.

"And to the best of my ability, preserve, protect and defend the Constitution of the United States." Plank said.

"And to the best of my ability, preserve, protect and defend the Constitution of the United States." Grumbly responded.

"So help me God." Plank concluded.

"So help me God." Grumbly affirmed while finishing the Presidential Oath of Office.

"Our prayers are with you Mr. President at this time of national crisis." Judge Plank added.

"Thank you Your Honor." President Grumbly said. Grumbly then began to address the nation. "My fellow Americans, an hour ago, we were attacked in manner that was unimaginable as well as unprecedented. Let me assure you that we will retaliate in a manner that is unprecedented and unimaginable as well. We will strike those who struck at the very heart of our nation. We will strike those who crippled our government, our military and defensive infrastructure. We will strike those who killed our leaders, our citizens and our soldiers. We will rebuild America to a nation that is greater than it previously was. We will rebuild our government and military and make it stronger than ever before. I command every American to rise up and fight the enemy and smote it from existence once and for all!" With that President Grumbly left the podium and began to draw up battle plans.

"I have a bad feeling about President Grumbly" Agent Bishop said.

"I don't trust him." Daley replied.

"Why?" Bishop inquired.

"He was out of Washington when the attacks took place. He was the only government official that survived this. I think he was in on it!" Ian shot back.

"I believe it!" Bishop said with conviction in his voice.

"I've worked with a lot of people in DC. I am very familiar with all of the players. Grumbly cannot be trusted. I am familiar with many of his dealings. They are not good to put it mildly." Daley argued.

The Galleria Mall which had been the sight of an almost overcrowded shopping hub a little more than an hour earlier was now the sight of untold carnage, destruction as well as terror on a scale in which no American had ever experienced. Blood, flesh, organs, tissue, bullets, shrapnel, shattered glass, twisted metal, charred furniture, merchandise, bodies, strewn Christmas gifts, and shopping bags were scattered throughout the mall. The once intact window panes of the stores were now removed due to sprayed gunfire. Merchandise including clothing as well as toys which had been previously intact had since been torn by bullets as well as bomb residue. The kiosks were peppered with bullets and covered with a mixture of blood and shattered merchandise. Christmas Village suffered from both extensive damage as well as casualties. The buildings, candy canes, gingerbread men, and statues were covered with bullets as well as blood. The Nativity scene suffered from extensive bullet, bomb and blood damage. It was the Victorian era caroler statues which gave the most haunting impression of the massacre that had just taken place. Despite being covered with blood, bullets and bomb residue, the carolers were singing "Joy to the world."

"This is where the worst carnage took place." Tim Lake began as he showed the FBI agents the carnage that took place in the food court of the Galleria "They were clearly going for the highest body count possible." Lake and the agents were surveying the scene while the emergency medical technicians were loading what little survivors there were from the carnage onto the ambulances. The Galleria Mall especially the food court looked like a scene reminiscent of two major terrorist attacks that took place. The first one occurred in Mumbai, India in November 2008, and the second at Westgate Mall in Nairobi, Kenya back in September 2013. Blood, body fragments which included bones, tissue and skin, pieces of clothing, bullets, bomb residue as well as pieces of the bombs were strewn throughout food court not to mention the rest of the mall. However, despite the grotesque scene not a single stomach of those who were working at the crime scene was present until they came upon the upper torsos of two young women who were torn from the rest of their bodies at the shoulder as well as the next. Most of their faces were charred, but their hair managed to stay intact. It was the names on the necklaces that confirmed the identities of Irene and Irma Daley which made Tim Lake's stomach turn. It would take several minutes before he could even begin to recover. Lake then said "My friend Ian Daley's been through too much. He lost his wife on 9/11 and now his two daughters. How much more can he take?" he continued as his voice began to choke up with emotion."

"Did you know the two girls?" an agent from the FBI inquired.

"Yes, I've known them since they were born." Lake replied.

"If you wish, we can let their father know." he offered.

"No. I must be the one who has to tell Ian about what happened." Tim said as he continued to pull himself together. Once lake pulled himself together he pulled out his cellphone and placed the most dreaded call that he had to make in his life to date. It would be to his close friend Ian Daley. Daley picked up the phone and said "Tim, are Irene and Irma alright."

"Ian, I need you to sit down." Lake began.

"What is it?" Daley replied as he began to sit down as he began to realize what was about to be said.

"Are you sitting down?" Tim asked.

"Yes." Ian responded as he quickly found a log to sit on. It was from a tree which had recently fallen down.

"Irene and Irma have passed away in the attacks." Lake said as he struggled to find the appropriate words to say.

"No!" Daley wailed as he began to sob uncontrollably while dropping the phone. Agent Bishop picked up the phone and said "We will be there for Ian."

"Thank you." Tim replied as he was now being motioned over to another area of the crime scene "Please have Ian call me when he can. I think the agents may have found some new evidence."

"First my wife was killed on 9/11 and now my little girls . . ." Daley sobbed "I must see them!" as he got up from the log he was sitting on and began to race towards the Galleria. Agent Bishop still held Daley's phone in his hand and he immediately placed a call to Tim Lake.

"Ian." Tim Lake began as he had quickly pressed the answer button.

"No it's me Agent Bishop from the FBI. Ian is racing over to see Irene and Irma. "Which entrance is he going to try to enter?"

"It looks like the main entrance." Bishop replied.

"I'm on my way." Lake said as he said to the investigators "I need to step away for a moment. My friend who I just told that we found his daughters' bodies is going to try to enter here." Lake now raced out of there in hopes of intercepting Daley.

Ian Daley continued to make his mad dash towards the Galleria as memories of events with Irene and Irma came to him in the form of flashbacks. The horror of the way that his twenty six year old twin daughters were killed enraged him completely. "*Those Arabs killed the three people who meant the most to me. They are going to pay for this!*" Ian thought as he was now near the main entrance of the Galleria. Tim Lake saw Ian from a distance and began to race out in an attempt to intercept Daley before he could go any further. Once the two were only a few feet away from each other, Ian asked "Where are Irene and Irma?"

"Don't go in there!" Lake yelled.

"I have to see my girls!" Daley screamed.

"Remember them the way they were, not the way they are now!" Tim shot back as he grabbed Ian "The only way we were able to quickly identify them was their necklaces!

Trust me; you don't want to see them! Especially right now! No parent should ever see how badly their children look after they were killed especially after an attack of this magnitude. Ian, you won't recognize them!" Tim pleaded as he and Agents Bishop, Downey and Frank Carter began to pull Ian back from entering the crime scene.

"I knew someone who saw the remains of her husband after the 9/11 attacks in the Pentagon. That was the lasting memories that they had of their loved on! Trust me; you don't need to see Irene and Irma the way they are now. Please remember them for the way they were. Please trust us on this!" Frank Carter pleased with Ian.

"Alright." Ian relented after he thought about it for a moment. Daley then said "Tim, I'm sorry."

"Ian, I understand. I've dealt with so many families of crime victims through the years. You have nothing to apologize for." Lake began as he added "If you ever need anything or to talk, please don't hesitate to call me even if it is in the middle of the night." he then offered. Tim then returned to the crime scene inside the Galleria Mall.

3:30pm

"We are now receiving reports of widespread looting throughout the country." began the WBMD reporter. "Several states are reporting that numerous cities as well as towns have had reports of supermarkets, stores and businesses broken into and merchandise has been taken. Rioting has broken out in cities such as Newark and Atlantic City both of which are in New Jersey, Charlotte and Raleigh in North Carolina, Atlanta, Orlando, Tampa Bay, New Orleans, Cleveland, Cincinnati, Louisville, Nashville, St. Louis, Dallas, Houston, Oklahoma City, Fargo, Phoenix, Santa Fe, Seattle, Portland, Sacramento and Oakland. Not only is there rioting but there is considerable widespread looting occurring as well. We are also receiving reports of numerous shooting as well as deaths as a result of these aforementioned events. The attacks have not only brought the United States to a complete standstill, but the attacks have also brought complete uncertainty to America as well given the untold damage to our infrastructure and military equipment, our weaponry and our nuclear power plants. This will likely result in a delay in any retaliatory strike that may take place. Also with the uncertainty with who will serve in the new government not to mention the actual government itself has brought uncertainty to the future direction that the United States will head in. There is no question that the hours and days to come the direction that this country may ultimately head in will begin to come into focus. There are also concerns that the attacks that have taken place may only be the beginning. There are strong indications that there may be more attacks to come in the coming hours if not in the coming days." he then paused and added "We can now confirm that there is also widespread rioting in Great Britain where their government and royalty were all decapitated in the attacks. At least ten million Britons were killed in the attacks and scores more injured. There is now a civil war raging between the British military and the Moslems who are in the British military as well as the Moslems who are residing in Great Britain. In Israel, battles are raging throughout the nation after members of the Israeli military were ambushed while heading to their respective military bases just as the attacks in both the United States and Great Britain took place. This civil war in Israel is taking place just as several Israeli cities and villages including Tel Aviv and Haifa were detonated with dirty bombs. In fact we are now receiving reports that every Palestinian citizen in Israel especially those who have resided in both the West Bank and the Gaza Strip have marched out as an army and are just beginning to engage in battle with the Israeli military who are just beginning to arrive at the scene of the firefights which are taking place throughout the country at this very hour."

"Has anyone in here read *Future Jihad* by Walid Phares?" Frank Carter asked those who were present with him.

"Yes." Agent Bishop replied "But the book did not cover scenarios of simultaneous attack in Great Britain as well as Israel."

"I noticed that as well." Carter noted while acknowledging what Agent Bishop had just said.

"I am familiar with the book." Agent Downey said.

"I thought about the scenario in the book where the September 11th attacks took place in 2008 instead of 2001." Ian Daley began "I am afraid that al-Qaeda got the inspiration to carry out today's attacks in part from that very scenario mentioned in *Future Jihad.* This is a classic example of what happens when we underestimate the enemy."

"This illustrates how once again terrorists read a book and then carry out a terrorist plot that was mentioned in a book." Agent Downey acknowledged.

"What have we come to as a country?" Frank Carter mused aloud while Agent Bishop took out his Federal Bureau of Investigation issued laptop and turned on the power. He now asked Agent Downey "What is Agent Bishop doing?"

"He is turning on his laptop. He usually does that in the middle of the conversation when a thought pops up in his mind." Agent Downey replied.

"I take it that the thought has to be something serious." Carter noted as Agent Downey nodded yes. "Is it up and running yet?" Agent Downey asked Agent Bishop in reference to Bishop's Federal Bureau of investigation issued laptop.

"Yes it is as of now." Agent Bishop replied as he now logged on to the Barron's website. He immediately clicked on the search icon for the shares of stock and first he typed in Cypress. CYP quickly cam up and Bishop was stunned that the company took a 10 point dip between one fifty and two pm eastern. Bishop then typed in PAO for Pan Arabian Oil and the stock rose fifteen dollars during that same period of time. "They not only attacked us, but they even manipulated the stock market as well." Agent Bishop then turned to Agent Downey and motioned him, Ian Daley and Frank Carter over and said "You need to see this." The three now raced over and looked at the information that was on Agent Bishop's Federal Bureau of investigation issued laptop.

"This could change everything." Agent Downey gasped as he looked at the transactions that were made by the Middle Eastern investors.

"The first two were made early this morning." Ian Daley observed "And the rest were made in the minutes leading up to the attacks."

"It looks like the investors were mainly based in Saudi Arabia as well as Afghanistan." Frank Carter remarked "There is definitely an al-Qaeda connection there. They think that the Saudi's will capitalize on the attacks and raise the price of oil knowing that we will be so desperate for it that we would pay anything for a barrel of oil I might add."

"This isn't the 1970's OPEC oil embargo." Ian Daley remarked in reference to the Organization of Petroleum Exporting Countries decision to jack up the price of oil exponentially after the Israel victory over Syria, Egypt, Jordan and Iraq in the Yom Kippur War of 1973 and the American support of Israel during the conflict that took place that October "This time we are so angry about how the Saudi's helped al-Qaeda today that we will not buy a drop of oil from them ever again. It is obvious that we and all of our allies will have to fight not only Afghanistan, but every Arab country that helped al-Qaeda carry out today's attacks including Saudi Arabia. We must not be afraid of inciting every Arab country as all as every Moslem to fight us. We would be showing the ultimate sign of weakness if we fail to do so!"

"But we may have to fight elements in our own country at the same time." Carter acknowledged "It is not only going to be an international war, but a domestic one I am afraid to say."

"I have no question that every freedom loving American who survived today's attack will immediately fight this war. America will never go down without a fight. I will definitely say this much for the United States of America." Agent Bishop stated.

"The four of us are definitely going to lead the charge." Agent Downey began "The four of us did more together that our entire government did combined for that matter and look where it led us to. We can definitely hold our heads up high knowing that we did everything we could to prevent this country from being attacked once more!" Downey stated emphatically while rallying the other three in the process. However the other three did not need to be rallied, they are already gearing up for the biggest fight of their lives as well as the life of the United States of America.

"We now have company!" an Israeli reservist began as he saw what seemed to be an army of Palestinians who were coming from the Gaza Strip. The Israeli reservists were beginning to get the upper hand on the Palestinian gun men who were gunning them down. The Palestinian mob quickly fired upon the Israeli reservists who were now being gunned down. "They're overpowering us once again!" he cried as the original group of Palestinians who initiated the massacre was once more getting the upper hand due to the reinforcements who were just arriving. The remnants of the Israeli reservists who had banded together as a fighting army were quickly mowed down. Then the Palestinian forces merged together and proceeded to the nearest Israeli military convoy while attacking villages along the way overpowering the residents in the process.

"You have your orders." the Iranian president said as he now ordered a nuclear strike on Israel which was still called Palestine by the Arabs. Within moments thirty missiles capped with nuclear warheads began to make their way to Israel while another thirty began to make their way towards the United State Military warships that were presently stationed in the Persian Gulf.

"Is this what I think it is?" began a marine who was on the USS Lafayette who was on its way to help rescue several ships which included the USS Sullivan, the USS Massachusetts and the USS Kennedy.

"It is." the Captain of the Lafayette replied as he belted out "Everyone! Man your battle stations! Iranian missiles are heading our way!"

At the same time, the militaries of Iraq, Syria, Jordan and Lebanon began to hurl their missiles in which some of them were capped with nuclear warheads at Israel. Defense Minister Shlivi quickly received a phone call from the military base in Northern Israel.

"Sir." the solider began "We have just detected missiles with quite possibly nuclear war heads coming from Lebanon, Syria, Jordan and Iran."

"We need to alert the defense minister at once." the commander replied. He proceeded to place the call to Defense Minister Shlivi.

"What is going on where you are Commander Herzberg?" Defense Minister Shlivi inquired.

"I have the Prime Minister on Skype." Shlivi began as he then said to Prime Minister Elihu "Sir, our commander of the Northern Israeli Army has just informed me of several missiles which are presumed to have nuclear warhead are heading our way from Iran, Iraq, Syria, Jordan as well as Lebanon. I recommend that we commence with the Samson Option at once." in reference to the Ancient Israeli judge who killed many Philistines as well as himself after a year of being blinded and imprisoned by them.

"You have my orders to commence Operation Samson at once." Prime Minister Elihu immediately commanded without any hesitation whatsoever given the circumstances. The United States and Great Britain were already devastated by terrorist attacks within the past hour and a half. There was no way that the nation of Israel would ever allow itself to suffer a similar fate without forcing its enemies to suffer the same fate at the same time.

"Commence the Samson Option immediately." Defense Minister Shlivi said not only to the Commander of the Northern Israeli Army but to every nuclear silo throughout Israel at the same time. With that the nuclear arsenal of Israel was unleashed upon Jordan, Lebanon, Iran, Iraq, Syria, Saudi Arabia and Afghanistan knowing that the attacks were coordinated in part by the latter two nations. Meanwhile the non-nuclear missiles were on their way to meet the nuclear warheads that were heading to Israel. The full scale war that has long been predicted for the Middle East was now well underway.

4:05pm

"They have company!" the Iranian soldier who was manning the radar in Qom began.

"What is it?" his commander quickly inquired.

"The Little Satan" the Iranian soldier began in reference to Israel "has fired at least seventy missiles towards not only our missiles but towards us, Jordan, Iraq, Syria and Lebanon and it looks like . . ." as the first Israeli missiles began to take out the warheads while some landed in Lebanon, Syria, Iraq and Saudi Arabia.

"Fire the other missiles!" the defense minister then commanded via Skype. With that more missiles from Iran were now on their way to Israel. Meanwhile one by one the first wave of nuclear warheads was being picked off by the anti-ballistic missiles that were supplied by both the United Sates as well as Great Britain. Meanwhile only three of the missiles were not picked off and two of them landed in the Mediterranean Sea while a third landed in central Israel. At the same time, a second wave of missiles from Iran, Iraq, Jordan, Syria and Lebanon were now on their way to Israel.

The firefight continued in the streets of Israel. As the soldiers heard the explosion that was in Central Israel, they said a mushroom cloud rise up from where the nuclear warhead from Iran landed. Now another round of air sirens quickly blared throughout Israel. This now signaled a second wave of missiles that were on their way to the Jewish State. Meanwhile both Israelis and Palestinians were now engaged in what has now become an all-out battle throughout Israel. The citizens from Jordan, Syria, Lebanon, Egypt and Saudi Arabia were now arriving in Israel as invading armies that were comprised of private citizens who were heavily armed like a militia would be. They now began to attack Israeli villages while joining in on the battles that were already taking place between the Palestinians as well as the Israelis. It was not only guns and machine guns that were being used, but hand grenades as well as Molotov cocktails were now being utilized in the battle while car bombs were now being used by all parties who were now involved in the fighting.

The Israeli military quickly learned about the second wave of nuclear warheads from the Arab nations. They Israeli military quickly fired off a second wave of a combination of nuclear warheads as well as intercontinental ballistic missiles towards their Arab enemies. At the same time, the remaining first wave of the nuclear warheads and anti-ballistic missiles as well as intercontinental warheads was now landing in Iraq, Iran, Saudi Arabia and Afghanistan.

“What was that?” Khalid Isawi bellowed as the explosion from the nuclear warhead was so loud that he could hear it at least one hundred miles away. He looked outside at saw a mushroom cloud from a distance. Just then he saw another warhead heading in his direction. His mouth now gaped open and he was frozen in fear. The missile carrying the nuclear warhead quickly grew larger by the second until it crashed into Isawi’s house killing Khalid, his family as well as destroying his crops which included heroin and opium at the same time.

One by one the USS Lafayette took out the Iranian silkworm missiles. The USS Ronald Reagan quickly joined in on the battle. Meanwhile another wave of missiles now crashed into the two warships. However the rest of the Silkworms were picked off by the two battleships as well as a third, the USS Nebraska in which a Silkworm barely missed it and crashed into the Persian Gulf. The three ships took out the rest of the Silkworms while the USS Lafayette and the USS Ronald Reagan proceeded to sink. Immediately the orders came from the USS Nebraska for its pilots to man their planes which would begin an all-out bombing campaign against Iran.

“Ishmael.” Alawi began “We’ve been hit in Afghanistan by the Zionists! Khalid Isawi has been killed! We have lost a good portion of our heroin and opium crops in the strikes!”

"Mecca and Medina have been both hit!" Ishmael Younis replied "Our people are calling for infidel blood to spill through the streets of Palestine, the United States and Great Britain! Every Moslem who has any salt is beginning to make their way to Israel to fight like we did in Afghanistan after the Soviet Union invaded it back in December, 1979."

"Every Moslem united as an army will smote those infidel Zionists from existence once and for all!" Alawi noted as he looked out of his window and saw the mushroom cloud still looming in Afghanistan.

"Our people are now marching to a car, a bus, a boat or even an airplane. Every Saudi who can do it is now on their way to Israel to fight in the war." Ishmael added. The Mahdi will soon meet us in Palestine to help us fight the final battle against the infidels once and for all." Younis stated in reference to the Mahdi who was known to the Sunni's as the Islamic messiah.

At the same time the American B-52's were in the process of pummeling Iran into submission. Meanwhile, the Iranian President said to his minister of defense "I have no question that the Twelfth Imam is on his way here now to help us smote the infidels from existence once and for all." The twelfth Imam was known to the Shi'ite Moslems as not only the hidden Imam, but the Shi'ite messiah. He had supposedly never passed away, but has since lived in hiding from the eighth century on. He would emerge at the end of the age according to Shi'ite tradition.

"He should be arriving at any time in order to take those B-52s down from the sky." the Iranian President began in reference to the Twelfth Imam as a bomb from one of the planes quickly landed on the building killing the Iranian President as well as the minister of defense not to mention countless other governmental ministers of Iran. Now the Iranian government was the third government of a nation that would be decapitated on this very day.

"Reports are now trickling in about a battle taking place in Iran where the United States military has sent in the B-52 fighter jets into the heart of Iran. As I report this development, Iran is being shelled and there are reports that the Iranian government has just been decapitated. I repeat we are now receiving unconfirmed reports that the Iranian government has been decapitated during an air strike by the United States Air Force within the past half hour." the WBMD reporter noted.

"Mr. President." Kirk Roberts began as he walked in on a phone call that President Grumbly was making.

"Let me call you back." Grumbly began as he added "Please let me know as soon as possible." While he quickly ended the call.

"The Air Force has just taken down the Iranian government." Roberts replied.

"Finally." Grumbly replied in a somewhat unenthusiastic tone. Roberts shot him a glance as asked "Are you alright?

You don't seem too happy that the Iranian government is no longer in existence."

"Kirk, I'm still in shock over the attacks." President Grumbly replied.

"Well get unshocked and fast. You're now the President of the United States of America. This country needs you to be strong and tough, not weak and in a state of shock. The people will pick up on that real quickly and you will not last long as president!" Roberts then paused and inquired "How soon until you give your next press briefing?"

"I will deliver another at 5pm Eastern." President Grumbly responded.

"It looks like those Zionists have crossed the line." Ishmael Younis began as he was chatting with Jabril Alawi via Yahoo messenger.

"What did they do?" Alawi inquired.

"They have invoked their Samson option." Younis began as he added "They are hurling all of their warheads towards us."

"Samson Option?" Alawi typed "Was he some great Zionist Soldier?"

"No." Ishmael typed back "Samson was an ancient judge of Israel who was blinded and imprisoned by the Philistines. A year after he was first captured he was brought out to the Philistine people and they made sport of him. Samson requested that he must stand between two pillars. The Philistines accommodated his request. Now Samson stood between the two pillars which were inside the Philistine Temple, he said a prayer and pushed both pillars over. The temple collapsed and everyone who was present at the temple including Samson was killed that day."

"So these Jews are now emulating Samson?" Khalid surmised.

"That would be correct." Ishmael noted as he then received a quick breaking news popup on the al-Jazeera website. He now read the latest news and quickly typed to Khalid "Jordan, Syria, Iraq, Iran and Lebanon have been hit with nuclear warheads." Meanwhile Younis received a phone call from the Head of Saudi Intelligence. "Hello." Ishmael began.

"There are some nuclear warheads heading our way. I need you to evacuate and head to an underground bunker!" he quickly ordered.

"I presume that at least four of the warheads are heading towards Mecca, Medina, Jidda and Riyadh?" Younis assumed.

"It looks that way." he started while quickly adding "You know that if Mecca and Medina are bombed that there will be an all-out war between us and the Jews. All Moslems regardless of whether they are Sunnis or Shi'ites will put aside our differences and band together as one faith and fight the Zionist aggressor terrorists and take them down once and for all. We must fight them regardless. They are a threat to us." the Head of Saudi intelligence noted. Meanwhile Ishmael typed the latest news to Jabril while another popup on Al-Jazeera quickly came up. Younis then typed to Alawi "Nuclear warheads are heading towards Afghanistan."

"They must have quickly figured this out." Jabril began to type "But how?' he wondered aloud.

"Someone in the Israeli government must have got a very quick read on this." Younis typed while he continued chatting with the Head of Saudi Intelligence. "There are now nuclear warheads that are going to Afghanistan."

"This is not only a declaration of war against every Arab, but one against every Moslem in the world as well. We need to push those Zionist infidels out of Palestine and drive them to the Mediterranean Sea in the process. That is the only way that those people will ever learn anything." He added.

"It is obvious that violence is the only language those Zionists know." Younis began as he the added "Considering they are the ones who perfected it into an art form."

"I am moving everyone to the underground bunker." Alawi typed. He then logged off and quickly went from door to door and alerted everyone about the impending nuclear strike against Afghanistan. Everyone inside the Alawi mansion whether they were family members or workers quickly moved to the underground bunker. Once the last person arrived they slammed the door shut and hunkered down, waiting for the impending nuclear strike to take place.

"How on earth did the security in the malls throughout the United States screw up this badly?' Investigator Rhodes inquired of Tim Lake.

"It is so ridiculous when there are laws which are in place to protect an individual's civil liberties in this country." Tim Lake began as he quickly quipped "Whatever happened to protecting the lives of Americans in general. If we had never allowed those bleeding heart liberals to chime in on how the United States should be run then we would not be in this mess right now!"

"It is very clear that the conservative right will definitely be chiming in on what you have said in the hours not to mention in the days, months as well as even years to come." Rhodes remarked "It looks like that we may be in for a curtailing of our rights as we know it."

"I am afraid that this is what we have come to as a nation." Lake began as he then continued "Look at how Israel has sacrificed their civil liberties in order to survive as a nation given the numerous terrorist attacks which has taken place inside their country. I have no question that once our government is rebuilt that they will use not only today's attacks as an example for curtailing our civil liberties but they will use Israel as an example for why limiting civil liberties works well for a nation."

"Remember that this is going to be a double edged sword. The terrorists will consider limiting our civil liberties as a victory for them." Rhodes said reminding Lake of the can of worms that he was opening.

"I know that this will receive a lot of opposition, but it is an option that we must seriously consider given the circumstances that have unfolded within the past two hours." Lake noted.

"Regardless of how this debate will play out we have much more important things to take care of first such as the rebuilding of our government, our military, our infrastructure and our economy. We must also retaliate against those who carried out the attacks against us as well as our allies. Once we take care of these very matters only then should we have a debate about whether we should limit civil liberties or not. It is only right that he hold this debate then given the much more important as well as pressing which are at hand as we speak." Rhodes noted. With that the two men walked through the Galleria Mall examining the carnage that had taken place only two hours earlier.

"What would be the latest?" Israeli Prime Minister Elihu asked Israeli Defense Minister Shlivi.

"Every member of the Israeli military as well as every Israeli citizen is now engaged in battle with the Palestinians as well as the other citizens of the neighboring Arab countries who are now marching into Israel to join the Palestinians in battle." Shlivi began as he then added "The Palestinians have both marched out of Gaza as well as the West Bank as two armies. We are dealing with every Palestinian man, woman and child engaging in battle with us right now. Have you had any luck in getting another country to help us since both the United States and Great Britain are unable to do so at this time?"

"I have had no luck what so ever." Elihu began "The only countries who have shown an interest are Japan and South Korea. Their defense ministers are trying to get approval from their respective leaders before committing any military personnel to the battle. As soon as they know, they will let us know. Do you have any nuclear warheads left?"

"Yes, we have a small handful." Shlivi began "There is a possibility that we may still have use for them in the future. We have already used eighty percent of our nuclear warheads tonight."

"Be prepared that we may have no choice but to use the rest of them soon enough." Prime Minister Elihu started "We have received some information from out katsas that the Russians as well as the Chinese have alerted the ministers of their nuclear facilities to get their nuclear warheads ready for use quite possibly within the next few hours."

"And for all of the times for our American and British friends to be crippled." Shlivi snarled "This would be the ideal time for them to use their nuclear warheads on not only our Arab enemies, but our Russian and Chinese enemies as well. By the way, we cannot rule out anything by the North Koreans and China for that matter. There is a concern that China may use this as an opportunity to seize Taiwan and North Korea to invade South Korea."

"I will alert the governments of South Korea and Taiwan at once." Prime Minister Elihu responded as he then proceeded to place a call to the leader of South Korea.

"Why hasn't the president ordered us to be on high alert?" Colonel Park Seung Wong inquired.

"He has been dealing with the other delegates at the Pacific Rim Trade Conference in Tokyo." Commander Chen Na Fu responded "I agree with you. We cannot count out the North Koreans from doing something." as the two men were patrolling the 38th Parallel while discussing the likelihood of an invasion by North Korea.

"They have a history of acting erratically." Col. Park acknowledged as he saw what seemed to be flares coming up from the sky.

"Everyone man your positions!" Commander Chen ordered his battalion.

"I wish to speak to the President of South Korea." Israeli Prime Minister Elihu began as he made contact with the government of South Korea.

"President Choi is in Tokyo attending the Pacific Rim Trade Conference Prime Minister Elihu. Is there problem?" the secretary asked.

"There is a possibility that North Korea may invade you." Elihu began as the secretary cut him off by saying "I will have President Choi call you immediately." He said as the call quickly came to an end.

"I wish to express on behalf of the nation of Taiwan my deepest condolences about the attacks." Ioki Chin said to his American visitor Steve Walters.

"It is such a tragedy about what has happened in my nation." Walters began as he then added "I have yet to hear back from our new president about how he would wish to proceed." The two men were employed by their respective governments and were laying what would be a potential strategic alliance between the two countries. The two men were now inside a government building in Taipei early Saturday morning. The streets were bustling with commuters heading to work while becoming quickly congested with both automobile traffic as well as crowds of people walking to work.

"As you can probably tell, we are greatly concerned with how the mainland will react to the attacks." Chin said in reference to China "We are concerned that they may invade us."

"Our military will be there for you." Walters replied as the two men now heard a very loud explosion. "I think there has been . . ." as the two men raced towards the window. The air sirens now blared extremely loud as they now saw other missiles from the mainland crashing into Taipei as well as other areas inside Taiwan ". . . an attack."

"We are now at war with the mainland." Chin acknowledged.

"This is outrageous!" President Choi shot back in response to the latest trade proposal that the government of China had just made "My people cannot absorb these taxes!"

"We cannot afford to keep losing money." Zhang Il Fong snarled.

"But you are a nation of billions." Choi began "We are only a nation of a million plus." He argued as there was a knock on the door. A security guard walked over to the South Korean president and handed him a note. Choi read it and said "Please excuse me for a moment. I have to make an emergency call." President Choi left the room and began to call Israeli Prime Minister Elihu when his cellphone began to ring. Choi answered the call and said "What is going on Defense Minister Foo?" noting the panic in his voice "I was about to call the Israeli prime minister."

"A dirty bomb has just been detonated inside Seoul!" Foo responded "The North has just lobbed a number of Taepodong VII missiles at us!"

"We must begin the retaliation at once." Choi ordered as he now turned on the News of Japan Network with was the Japanese equivalent of CNN. The latest news made Choi's mouth drop.

"As the North Koreans have begun their invasion of South Korea, China lobbed several missiles into Taiwan destroying Taipei as well as several surrounding villages. This coming on the heels of the attacks in America, Great Britain and Israel."

"I recommend that you do not return here anytime soon." Defense Minister Foo suggested "Your plane will be shot down by the North if you try to return. We need you alive so you can lead us into battle."

"I must be with my people." Choi stated sternly as he now saw a Taepodong VII missile head towards Tokyo. Before Choi could even begin to get out of the room, the missile crashed into the building killing all who were inside. Meanwhile Defense Minister Foo's balance was thrown off and he fell to the ground given the severity of the explosion.

"What happened?" asked the assistant Defense Minister Oke.

"If it is what I think it is, we must prepare to swear in a new president as soon as possible." Foo stated as he quickly added "We need to get everyone to the bunkers at once." he added in reference to every governmental official in North Korea as the air sirens were blaring almost non-stop as one missile after another was being hurled at Seoul as well as the rest of North Korea. Just then a series of missiles were now being lobbed towards Tokyo, Alaska, Hawaii and the west coast of the United States.

"Mr. President!" Kirk Roberts began as he was now shocked over the unconfirmed reports that he had just received.

"What is it Kirk?" President Grumbly inquired.

"China is invading Taiwan, North Korea has not only invaded South Korea, but has lobbed their Tapeodong VII missiles which has struck Seoul, Tokyo, Alaska, Hawaii and the west coast!"

"What are we coming to?" President Grumbly replied as he put his head in his hands "I need to speak to Commander Southworth at once!" in reference to the commander of the Pacific Fleet.

"Commander Southworth was killed when one of the missiles from China landed on the USS Hawaii." Roberts responded while noting the relative indifference in the president's tone and mannerisms at the same time.

"Who is next in command?" Grumbly barked as he was now demanding to know what was going on.

"The entire Pacific fleet was taken out by the missiles from North Korea and China." Kirk added.

"Then who do we turn to for military advice?" President Grumbly inquired as Roberts continued to pick up on what was clearly becoming a nonchalant attitude towards the attacks.

"You're the president. You can figure that one out for yourself." Roberts snarled as he walked out of the room while adding "You have an address to make to the American people at 5. Try to show some emotion."

4:30pm

One by one, the missiles from North Korea were landing at the various population centers of South Korea as well as the strategic South Korean military bases and instillations. Meanwhile the rest of South Korea was quickly mobilizing as a civilian army grabbing whatever weapons that were available. Then they began to gather in groups which quickly merged together as they saw other groups of South Koreans who were also going to invade North Korea. At the same time, whatever was left of the South Korean and American military presence at the 38th Parallel proceeded to enter North Korea. Much to their surprise, the North Korean citizens were greeting the South Koreans the way an occupied country would greet a liberating army. It was scenes like this that were becoming commonplace in the southern part of North Korea. Meanwhile, several members of the South Korean and American military were now reporting these developments to their superiors.

"What is your take on the defection of the North Korean citizens to our side?" the South Korean admiral began. He was now serving as the acting commander of the South

Korean military after the attacks took out most of the military command of South Korea.

"I would not trust them." the American General of the 38th Parallel replied "It may be a ruse."

"Then how do you explain a few thousand North Koreans who were quick to welcome us as a liberating force?" He Nam Xiang mused aloud.

"Have you met any resistance so far?" General Ford inquired.

"Very few if any." He added.

"I need to have a word in private with General Ford for a moment." Colonel Dawson suggested. With that the teleconference came to a brief halt. Colonel Dawson then said to General Ford "Sir, I think the North Korean defectors who have surrendered are sincere."

"What makes you so sure?" General Ford inquired.

"Of all who have surrendered so far, there were very few of those who didn't surrender who actually fought our forces. I say we question those who have surrendered so far. If their stories are consistent, then we must consider believing that they are sincere in defecting."

"Very well then." Ford began "Just be prepared in case they are actually fighting for the North Koreans."

"Yes sir." Dawson responded as the two then resumed the teleconference.

"I suggest that you question the defectors to make sure that their stories are the same. Just act as though they may not be sincere." General Ford ordered Admiral He.

"It is now safe to say that ten thousand North Koreans have defected." Admiral He responded "I am now becoming concerned that we may have a much bigger humanitarian crisis than we previously thought." He noted in reference to the attacks as well as the surrender of numerous North Korean citizens. With that those present at the meeting quickly began to make contingency plans for how to properly handle tens or even hundreds of thousands of North Korean defectors.

The Chinese military quickly took over the Spratley Islands as well as the oil pipeline in the Pacific Ocean. They were now entering Taiwan without much resistance from the Taiwanese military as well as its citizens. Meanwhile the nearest American warships were only hours away from the area. The Chinese military were now quickly mowing down those who were giving the Chinese military resistance. It was quickly becoming clear depending on the point of view that either the Chinese or the rest of the world had, whether China was taking back its territory or they were overrunning Taiwan and then annexing it in the process.

5:00pm

"My fellow Americans." President Nathan Grumbly began "In the past three hours since the attacks on the United States, Great Britain as well as Israel, we are beginning to confirm that it was a multi-national plot coordinated by Saudi Arabia, Afghanistan, Iran, Iraq, Jordan, Syria and Lebanon. The terrorist group al-Qaeda recruited the aforementioned nations to help them carry out this dastardly as well as diabolical attack against our nations. At this hour the United States government is not only rebuilding the government as well as our military, but our infrastructure as well. The process to inspect our weaponry to ensure that they are ready to be used in a military strike is underway as I address you. Also, we are receiving even more disturbing news that China is about to annex Taiwan after invading it within the past hour. North Korea has not only lobbed its nuclear warheads at South Korea, Japan, Alaska, Hawaii and the West Coast of the United States with help from China. It is these multipronged attacks by this growing multinational coalition against the United States and its allies that is the highest threat to the security of the United States and its allies." Grumbly then paused and added "However, I cannot discuss anything else with you at this time given the fact that it would compromise national security." With that Grumbly ended his presidential briefing and went back into his bombproof shelter which was outside Washington, DC.

"That was very comforting to know." Ian Daley said with a sarcastic tone in his voice.

"Anyone could have told us that." Frank Carter replied is contempt crept into his voice.

"Then why is President Grumbly taking his time rebuilding the government as well as inspecting the weapons and making sure that they are ready for use?" Agent Bishop inquired.

"Other than the fact that it could be very time consuming to do all of these tasks that the president has just mentioned, I have no clue." Agent Downey conceded while he was trying to keep an open mind while he was in denial that the terrorist attacks could be an inside job.

"I am beginning to think that they may have been an inside job in part." Ian Daley mused aloud.

"Inside job?" Agent Downey blurted as he realized that Daley had said what he was in denial of thinking a second ago "I hate to say this, but that thought has crossed my mind too. I know it sounds very farfetched, but with the assassination of Eric Watson, the sudden transactions involving Cypress and Pan Arabian stock just before the attacks took place and not to mention the recount as well as the voter tampering involving the voting machine that were produced by Cypress

Inc." he rambled as he was beginning to know that it was a very good possibility that this could very well be the case.

"Once you look at what Agent Downey just mentioned as well as the attacks here, Great Britain and Israel I am sure that any thinking individual would at the very least consider the possibility right about now." Agent Bishop noted.

"You know this will incite a revolution within this country at the very least." Frank Carter added as he then said "Between the attacks and the story about the Democrats being involved in the voter tampering in order to make the Republicans look bad, this will push everyone over the edge as far as I am concerned."

"I agree." Ian Daley noted "I would definitely run the story on Sunday. The American people have a right to know what is really going on no matter how devastating it is to hear."

"This could very explain how the attacks took place as well as why." Agent Bishop stated as the four continued on with their conversation.

"How much longer can we hold them off?" a member of the Israeli reserves asked as he and his fellow reservists were fighting not only the Palestinians, but also what was becoming a multi-national army of citizens from various Middle Eastern countries. This battle was now taking place along the main road to Jerusalem.

"I'm not sure!" a second reservist replied as they were now resorting to guerilla warfare in an attempt to put down the Palestinians as well as the others at the same time.

"We need to find an opening and fast!" bellowed a third reserve as people from both sides went from being quickly mowed down to being gradually being mowed down. They were now on the brink of running out of weapons other than knives. Meanwhile the fighting raged on until the last weapons other than their knives were used. With that the biggest street battle that the world has ever experiences was now well under way.

"Come on!" bellowed the British solder as he was now engaging with his battalion in battle with his Islamic counterparts. They were trying to get through the rubble of a building in a town which was miles away from London in order to eliminate the British soldiers of the Islamic faith.

"Just why did allow those Moslems into this country to begin with?" a second British soldier mused aloud.

"I have wondered that myself." he noted while adding "And why were they even allowed into our military. These things I definitely want to know. There has to be a law that states no Moslems allowed in Great Britain as well as our army!" Meanwhile they were able to get halfway through the rubble when they saw where the grenades were coming from. Just then the British soldiers quickly began to mow down the al-Qaeda operatives who had been serving in the British military. Gradually the al-Qaeda soldiers were being killed while the British were losing their soldiers in lesser numbers. The war continued to rage on until the British soldiers would clearly have an advantage. With that the rest of the al-Qaeda soldiers were killed with relative ease.

The battled raged on in Jerusalem as Moslems and Jews were killing one another. Meanwhile the Christians joined in with the Jews for the most part while a small sect of Christians decided to live out their anti-Semitic as well as their anti-Moslem tendencies. They decided to kill both the Jews and the Moslems in order to claim the city of Jerusalem in the name of Christianity. One by one the renegade Christian sect would lay in wait in a separate area inside Jerusalem and waited for the Jews and the Moslems to show themselves in battle.

"There they are!" one Christian remarked to another while they now witnessed Moslems and Jews engaging in gun battle inn one of the main streets of Jerusalem. The two Christian renegades knew that this was their opportunity to hasten the Second Coming of Christ. They took out their hand grenades and hurled it towards the two groups of combatants. Explosions quickly took place at the center of where each group was stationed in their battle with the other religion.

"Oy Vey!" a Jewish fighter exploded as they now quickly dispersed while fighting a band of Palestinian militants. They dispersed while firing in both the direction of where the Palestinians were firing their weapons as well as their hand grenades at. The Jews assumed that the Palestinians were throwing their hand grenades at the Jews.

"This is a new low as far as I am concerned!" another Jewish resident of Jerusalem bellowed as they fired their weapons in the direction that the hand grenades came from.

"Those Jews just fired their hand grenades at us from over there!" a Palestinian male screamed as he and his comrades quickly fled the scene while firing their guns as well as their grenades in the direction of both where the gunfire came from as well as the hand grenades. They now saw smoke where the Jews had previously positioned themselves in their battle with the Palestinians.

"Those grenades exploded where the Zionist pigs were firing their weapons at us!' a second Palestinian male noted.

"I don't think it was the Jews attacking us." the first Palestinian male began.

"What do you mean by that?" blurted the second Palestinian male.

"I don't think those Zionist invaders would sacrifice some of their own given how they need everyone to fight us." the first Palestinian male noted.

"Either this is a bold ruse or we are being attacked by a third group." the second Palestinian surmised as he added "Those Christian pigs!' he bellowed as they now decided to attack the Christians as well as the Jews. It was now becoming very evident that the battle not only for the city of Jerusalem but the entire nation of Israel was now being fought by Christians, Jews and Moslems in order to claim it for their own respective religion.

"What?" blurted Tim Lake as he was now told for the first time about the other attacks that took place not only in the United States, but also in Great Britain as well as Israel.

"I am afraid that the Galleria was only a small front in what has become a much larger game plan that is being executed not only by al-Qaeda, Hamas and Hezbollah but also several Arab governments at this hour." Investigator Rhodes acknowledged "Those elements that I have just mentioned have not only attacked us, but Great Britain as Israel at the same time."

"Didn't it ever occur to you that this country and Great Britain had to be attacked and put out of commission so that they can then attack Israel knowing that there would be little to no resistance to them at all." Lake observed.

"That thought has crossed my mind." Rhodes stated "This does make a lot of sense to me."

"I need to call my friend in Homeland Security and let him know about this at once." Lake said as he then placed a call to Ian Daley. Daley answered it by saying "Hello." while feeling very winded.

"Ian, I think I may have something for you." Tim began.

"What is it?" Daley inquired.

"It looks like that they attacked us as well as Great Britain so that both country would be unable to assist Israel if at all in their war with the Arabs countries as well as al-Qaeda, Hezbollah and Hamas. They knew that once the United States and Great Britain were attacked in such a devastating manner that the path the strike Israel would be very easy knowing that Israel would not be able to receive help from its two most powerful allies." Lake suggested.

"We have been looking into this angle that you just brought up." Daley began "With the information that you just brought up we can definitely validate this theory." He then paused and continued on "Are there any new developments at the Galleria?"

"We are still counting the casualties." Lake started "There may be at least two thousand killed today. We won't know for sure until we completely go over the mall though. Also we are trying to get our auxiliary cameras up and running as well. We think that there may be more evidence that wasn't detected in the time leading up to the attack here. There is a very strong possibility that this may have been an inside job." Tim dreaded as he uttered those very words.

"There is some uncorroborated evidence that we've uncovered which may indicate that some members of the government as well as at least one private corporation that may have played a role in the attacks." Daley acknowledged "However I cannot prove it at this time though."

"I take it that the corporation may be Cypress." Lake surmised.

"Ahem." Daley sounded as he cleared his throat. This was a signal that the two men had agreed upon years ago that if one asked the question and neither one could answer that they would clear their throat sometime right after the question was asked as a signal that the response was yes. "No."

"I see." Lake replied as he now began to realize the potentially far reaching implications of the investigation not only into the terrorist attacks, but also quite possibly into the presidential recount that was ongoing.

The Chinese government began to raise the Chinese flag throughout Taiwan. For the first time since 1949 there would be a unified China. The Chinese Premier Yu Chow Yan began to address the citizens of Taiwan "For the first time in almost seventy five years, the Chinese government addresses the residents of Formosa Island. You thought that you may break away from us and that we would never reclaim you as our own. You were wrong. Formosa Island is once more a part of China and will remain so forever. Do not try to break away from us since any attempt that you may make will quickly become squashed. Your so-called government since 1949 no longer exists. The traitors to Mother China have been executed for their crimes against us. We will execute any and all traitors against us in the future." Yan began as he continued on with his rousing address to Formosa Island which until two hours ago was known as Taiwan.

The defections continued in en masse in North Korea. As the South Korean army continued their advance, the Japanese military began to bomb Pyongyang in retaliation for the nuclear strike against Tokyo only hours earlier. Meanwhile, as the North Korean citizens surrendered in large numbers to the South Korean army, the North Korean government was quickly becoming disturbed by the reports.

"Is this true that our citizens are defecting to North Korea in large numbers?" Kim Jong Un inquired.

"I am afraid so." King Song Park replied as the North Korean Defense Secretary continued "I have been receiving continuous reports about this in the past few hours."

"We carried out this invasion for them and look how they thank us!" Kim Jong Un snarled "Besides, Japan has damaged our capital. I command that the missiles are to be launched continuously at South Korea and Japan while a few are lodged at the United States."

"Yes sir." Park replied as he relayed the orders. With that a series of Taepodong VII missiles were quickly fired off in the direction of North Korea, Japan and the United States.

"More missiles are now being fired towards us!" Defense Minister Fu began as the air raid sirens blared "Deploy not only the anti-aircraft missiles, but also bomb Pyongyang until it no longer exists!" Just then the anti-aircraft missiles were quickly fired. Several of the missiles destroyed the Taepodong VII missiles while the rest of them either left South Korean airspace or landed in South Korea. Meanwhile the missiles from South Korea began to land in Pyongyang causing unprecedented damage to the city in which it quickly became virtually uninhabitable.

“What is the latest on the damage?” Kim Jung Un began as another missile from South Korea crashed above the underground bunker that he was in at the present moment. The impact was so hard that the ground began to cave in killing the North Korean dictator and those who were present. The remnants of the South Korean government had the phone wiretapped and with that they began to celebrate the fact that there would now be a unified Korea.

6:00pm

"It is now six o'clock on the East Coast." the WBMD-TV news anchor from Baltimore began "Just yesterday, a nation was celebrating Thanksgiving. Today it is a period of grave and unparalleled mourning. A tragedy of monumental proportions, one that has never taken place until today took place only four hours ago. Tens of millions were killed after fifty four passenger planes crashed into the places such as the Sears Tower, The Empire State Building, the Pentagon, the White House, the U.S. Congress, the CIA and FBI headquarters, targets in Las Vegas, Los Angeles, Boston, and Miami as well as nuclear power plants, ports and airports. Trucks have exploded in front of local FBI as well as federal buildings while security units were mobilizing to be deployed. We are also receiving reports where across the nation, shopping malls are being massacred, and the main hubs of the national media have been attacked. There has been an all-out cyber-attack as well. Twelve U.S. task forces, the main military instillations as well as bases are being attacked. Terrorists using dirty bombs as well as suicide bombers attacking several U.S. cities. New York, Boston, Philadelphia, Washington, Charlotte, Atlanta, Miami, Orlando, New Orleans, Nashville,

Indianapolis, Chicago, Minneapolis, St. Paul, Kansas City, St. Louis, Las Vegas, Dallas, Houston, Oklahoma City, Denver, Phoenix, Los Angeles, San Francisco, San Diego, Sacramento, Portland and Seattle are among those cities that have been attacked. This unprecedented act of terrorism coming during a presidential recount that may further divide America. The Presidential and Vice Presidential candidates for both parties we can now confirm have been assassinated in the attacks." The reporter briefly paused and then added "The rioting has escalated throughout America since the attacks took place only four hours ago. The horror which one would expect from a Hollywood movie or even a novel has come to life in ways that were unseen here until early this afternoon. In fact some are saying that it was these types of storylines both from Hollywood as well as best-selling novels which may have ultimately influenced al-Qaeda to carry out today's attacks. We are now brining in a psychologist as well as a criminologist from a local university who will explain how Hollywood and novels may have influenced al-Qaeda to attack this country today." He then took a deep breath and now continued on "And the United States of America was not the only nation that was attacked at two o'clock eastern time this afternoon. In Great Britain, the Parliament Building as well as Buckingham Palace, Big Ben and the Tower of London were attacked and reduced to rubble. At the same time, suicide bombers detonated themselves inside cafes, restaurants as well as pubs. Dirty bombs were detonated in London, Manchester, Glasgow, Liverpool and several other cities and towns. While this first wave of attacks were taking place inside Great Britain, Islamic soldiers in the British army as well as Islamic citizens of great Britain rose up and revolted against the British military thus causing a civil war to take place that is still raging on at this hour. While the massive carnage took place in both the United States and Great Britain where their governments were also decapitated, Israel was attacked also at the same time. While the Israel government escapes decapitation, dirty bombs were detonated in Tel Aviv, Haifa, Jaffa as well as several other Israeli cities and towns. The only major city that was not detonated by a dirty bomb was Jerusalem where every Jewish, Moslem and Christian citizen are fighting once another at this very moment for control of the Holy City that is sacred to the three monotheolic religions, Judaism, Christianity as well as Islam. Also, Palestinians were picking off Jewish military members and reservists with rifles and automatic weapons while that were racing to their nearest military stations in order to prepare for battle."

"How come no one here is surprised by this?" Agent Bishop stated "Wait until they mention that a non-fiction book resulted in today's attack." Bishop added in reference to *Future Jihad* by Walid Phares.

"There has always been a concern that Hollywood and authors would influence a terrorist group to carry out an attack against us." Ian Daley began "Look at the 1994 Tom Clancy novel *Debt of Honor*. Writing about a hijacked plane crashing into the U. S. Capital building influenced al-Qaeda to hijack those planes and crash them into the World Trade Center, the

Pentagon and the White House. Luckily the White House attack was averted until today. Now non-fiction books have become inspirational to terrorists. What have we come to as a nation?"

"Back up for a moment. How do you know that it was the White House that the September 11th hijackers intended to crash Flight 93 into?" Frank Carter started "I thought it was the Capital."

"We always kept that quiet. We did not want to cause further panic." Daley said.

"There was always a question among the public about where Flight 93 was supposed to crash into." Carter began "That can definitely bring this debate to closure."

"I highly recommend that you keep this quiet for reasons pertaining to national security." Daley ordered Carter.

"I will do so unless you tell me otherwise." Frank conceded.

"It's hard to suppress the storylines by Hollywood as well as the authors who write these kinds of novels." Agent Downey began "We are working in part to defend their right to produce these types of stories and yet look where that got us."

"I hope that today curtails this phenomenon considerably if not all together." Ian Daley started "That has resulted in three members of my family getting killed in terrorist attacks. This has to end now!"

"I'm afraid that these sorts of stories will never be completely suppressed from being told." Frank Carter began

"There is someone out there who will always tell this type of story. The sad part is that their right to do so is protected in the Constitution. This will result in the suppression of civil liberties. It would begin with the preventing of authors to write disaster stories and Hollywood to make disaster movies. Our freedom as a nation will gradually go downhill until the United States is no longer a democracy. That is exactly what al-Qaeda and the other terrorist groups want us to do. They will win if we begin to curtail our civil liberties as well as our civil rights for that matter." he implored the others.

"No one wants to see our democracy to cease to exist." Agent Bishop began "It has been dealt a very severe blow this afternoon. We can rise above it though."

"How can we rise above this as a nation when our president is not lifting a finger to help this nation fight back?" Agent Downey mused.

"I am not a Nate Grumbly fan." Ian Daley began "However one hope that he is working behind the scenes in order to rebuild the government while making battle plans to strike back against al-Qaeda."

"From what we are seeing, that is up for debate." Frank Carter noted "I don't think Grumbly is doing a thing to help this country. If anything I think he is up to something and it's not good."

"We are now receiving breaking news on the other two fronts. First, we are receiving unconfirmed reports that the government of North Korea has been decapitated. If these reports are confirmed as true then for the first time since 1950 there will be a unified Korea. Also additional North Korean missiles have landed not only in South Korea, but in Japan as well as Honolulu, Maui, Anchorage, Juneau, Fairbanks, Spokane, Eugene, San Francisco, Phoenix and Yuma. If South Korea in fact has won the war, it will have achieved victory at a very huge price. That price would be the deaths of a majority of its citizens. Meanwhile the Chinese flags have been raised throughout Taiwan. Chinese Premier Yu Chow Yan has been addressing the citizens of what used to be known as Taiwan for the past twenty minutes. Here is live coverage of that address. "The re-Chinatization of Formosa Island has begun. You are no longer known as Taiwan. You are once more Chinese citizens. I wish to say to the United States, Russia and any of their allies that any attempt to invade Formosa Island as a liberating army will be considered an attack on China and will be dealt with the most punishing response that we will deliver."

"How do you want to proceed Mr. President?" Grumbly's chief of staff inquired.

"I am still trying to locate the highest ranking members of each branch of the military." Grumbly began "I must know that exact military capabilities that we have remaining after the attacks."

"Sir, that could take quite a while and time is of the essence." Chief of Staff Roberts replied.

"Yes, I am well aware of it. I refuse to commit to using weapons that may no longer be operable!" President Grumbly shot back.

"Still we need to start making plans. The public is not only demanding revenge but carrying it out against Arab-Americans as we speak." Roberts added "You need to step up and do something."

"What on earth do you think I have been doing, playing solitaire?" Grumbly snarled sarcastically.

"This is not a time for jokes Mr. President." Chief of Staff Roberts exploded.

"And this is not a time for you to question my authority not to mention question my ability as president. We have suffered an attack unlike any other nation has experienced. I want to strike back as soon as possible, but I am concerned that if we strike back immediately that our weapons may not be working properly. This alone would defeat the purpose of retaliation!" Grumbly bellowed as his tirade was well underway "If you have any ideas about what to do, I would like to hear them immediately if not, shut up and let me do my job!"

"Did you get everything up and running?" Tim Lake asked in reference to the damaged computer screens.

"Yes I did." the technician replied as he began to show the recordings from the various cameras inside the mall. Soon they noticed a number of Arab Americans entering the mall and then separating. Later on they left the mall and stayed in their cars for a prolonged period of time. Then they took out another large shopping bag and brought their weapons to the mall in those bags and began to carry out the attack. Tim Lake kept staring at the screens in complete disbelief. "So this is why the guy who was watching the screen to lunch around 1:30 this afternoon." Tim Lake immediately picked up the phone and placed a call to Ian Daley. Daley picked up the phone and said "Yes Tim."

"Ian." Tim Lake began "I think we may have found the persons who carried this out. They blew themselves up during the attack."

"Another cowardly act by a bunch of cowards!" Daley exploded.

"They believe that they are doing it for religious reasons, but their actions are deplorable." Lake began as he quickly changed the subject "Would you like to talk about what happened?"

"I have so much to say that it will take quite a while." Ian began as he continued "I worked in a department is was created as a result of a terrorist attack which killed my wife. They were supposed to prevent another attack from occurring, but they failed miserably. My little girls were killed because of their lazy, incompetent policies. They would still be alive if the government had made better planning instead of creating another department which ultimately was not only cut due to budget restraints, but by bureaucratic red tape at the same time."

"Is that what has really been going on in Washington?" Tim asked.

"Tim this is the tip of the iceberg. I am only just beginning to tell it as it is." Daley continued "Wolcott is the worst president we have had since George W. Bush and believe me I have seen some morons occupy the Oval Office since especially Obama. Do we have any great statesman left in the United States or have they been relegated to a bygone era in American history?"

"I'm sure there are some who are still around." Lake began as Daley cut him off "But if there are any I am sure that none of them desire to become president knowing the mess that they would inherit."

"The United States didn't get into the mess overnight and it shouldn't be expected to get out of this mess overnight. It's going to take a lot of time just to get out of it. No one should ever think that a president can get a nation out of a mess in one or even two terms for that matter. If anything it would take two presidents who would serve two terms each just to make it happen." Lake argued.

"President Clinton brought the United States from a record deficit to a record surplus in the course of eight years." Ian recalled.

"But that is not the case today. The deficit is worse now than it was when Clinton first became president." Tim acknowledged "Too much was expected out of President Obama to begin with. There was no way that he could follow through on every campaign promise that he made."

"Then he should have never made those promises to begin with." Ian noted "It has been one mistake after another for the

American presidency for years. Look what it has resulted in. We let our guards down once again and now we're paying the price once more because of it! I have to end this call, I'm too riled up to even continue on talking." Ian added as he hung up the phone.

"Not a peep from the new president of the infidels." Jabril Alawi said to Ishmael Younis in reference to President Nathan Grumbly's inaction when it came to responding to the terrorist attacks that took place only four hours earlier. "We definitely scared not only the infidels, but their cowardly leader at the same time. We have not only brought them to their knees but kicked them to the ground at the same time with no hopes of them ever getting up again!"

"The infidels will never rise again." Younis began as he then added "They are definitely not proud to be Americans right now." he said as he recalled the 1984 hit song *I'm Proud to be an American* by Lee Greenwood that was played virtually non-stop not only after 9/11 in order to rally Americans after the devastating terrorist attacks in New York and Washington, but also Osama bin Laden was killed in May 2011.

"I have no question that they won't be able to retaliate against as this time." Alawi proclaimed.

"Even their allies or what is left of them would not be able retaliate knowing that it would be a losing cause." Younis began as he quickly added "We would be able to successfully defeat both Israel as well as Great Britain so far without putting in much effort."

The battle in Jerusalem continued to rage on as both sides in the battle were now in what was becoming a stalemate. The battle was now quickly at a standstill with both sides now hunkering down and lying in wait for the next round to begin.

"How much longer until we can start to take them down once and for all?" asked a Jewish resident of Jerusalem.

"We just have to wait for the order." a second Jewish resident replied.

"But when?" the first complained.

"Be patient, it is coming." the second said while trying to calmly reassured the first.

"Our ahnillation will come if we don't act now!" the first shot back as he began to leap out of his post while the second now tacked him very quickly "Remember we wait!" he said over and over again until the first was calmed down enough that we would listen to what the second was saying to him. Just then the Palestinian gunmen saw them and began to open fire. The Jewish residents of Jerusalem quickly fired off several rounds at the Palestinians in turn. It was a firefight which quickly became very fierce.

"Look out!' the first now bellowed to the second as a hand grenade was thrown in their direction. They quickly ran and were able to avoid the explosion in the process. They continued on firing off what would become several rounds of bullets in the direction of the Palestinian soldiers taking out most of them in the process. Just then the Jewish residents saw the Palestinian residents converge upon them with their machine guns drawn. The Jews quickly fired off several rounds into the Palestinians taking them out completely. Now they were very relieved that once cluster of Palestinian guerillas were taken down, but there were several more to go. This occurring as even more Palestinians and Arabs from Jordan were now converging upon the Holy City with the intentions of liberating it from the Zionist occupiers.

"We are now receiving reports that a third Israeli nuclear warhead has landed in Saudi Arabia. This time it landed in Riyadh after similar strikes in both Mecca in Medina." began the reporter from Al-Jazeera "From all accounts the Saudi Government has been decapitated in the strike. If these reports are confirmed Saudi Arabia would become the fourth country today in which their entire governments have been decapitated after an attack following the United States, Great Britain as well as Iran." Now he was reading another story which just broke out loud "There are now unconfirmed reports that the North Korean government has been decapitated. If this is confirmed, there will be a total of five governments which have been decapitated in the past few hours."

"Now is the hour for revenge!" Ishmael Younis began as he was calling for an all-out attack against Israel "Those Zionists must pay the ultimate price for what they have done to our people!" Younis barked. He had now become the unofficial leader of Saudi Arabia as of this hour. He now continued as he addressed the Saudi people "We all must go to Israel as an army and liberate Palestine for the Palestinian people!" Millions of Saudi's did not need to heed Younis' call since they were already on their way to Israel in order to retaliate for the nuclear warheads that took out Mecca, Medina as well as Riyadh. Once Younis was finished with his speech, he made his way over to the Head of the Saudi Intelligence Community and asked "Would we have more than enough soldiers to take out Israel and return it to the Palestinian people once and for all?"

"Absolutely." the Head of Saudi Intelligence replied as he quickly added "And we will still have more than enough soldiers who will be more than able to maintain order here while the war is going on."

"How bad is the damage from the nuclear strikes on Mecca, Medina and Riyadh?" Younis now inquired.

"Mecca and Medina suffered significant damage. The Grand Mosque in Mecca is no more." he frowned "We must be quick in delivering any blows to the Jewish people.' The Head of Saudi Intelligence now cautioned "Not only will we have many of our brothers fighting alongside fellow Moslems and Palestinians, but we must have some sort of coordinated effort as well as unity among all Moslem soldiers who are fighting for Palestine."

"I have no question that the destruction of Israel is enough of a reason to bring about complete unity among all of the freedom fighters who are converging upon Palestine at this very moment.

Rescue workers were now aiding victims of the London attacks. Meanwhile the other rescue workers were coming to the aid of those who were attacked throughout Great Britain. They were going to the areas of London where the nuclear radiation had yet to affect the population of London. Most of the center of London was reduced to ruins while vaporized impressions of people replaced the actual people who are standing in the same spots when the dirty bomb was detonated not only in London but throughout Great Britain as well. The sight of most of London, England being reduced to rubble was a very heartbreaking sight. Millions by millions of people throughout the world had converged upon London throughout history. For one of the most famous cities in the world to practically no longer exist as it once was very troubling not to mention very disturbing as well as very depressing. The same could go for cities like New York City, Boston, Los Angeles as well as Las Vegas all of which were in the United States. Billions of people throughout the world had a lot of trouble comprehending that several cities not only in the western hemisphere, but those cities which were not only in Israel, but in the Middle East as well were also virtually destroyed. This had be among the saddest feeling throughout the world that some of its most famous and beautiful cities in the world had only existed only hours earlier until a group of Islamic fanatics decided that it was time to destroy them in the name of Islam. The Israelis in turn decided that it was time to destroy the Arab cities in the name of protecting the Jewish state of Israel in retaliation for the terrorist attacks not only in Israel, but in the United States as well as Great Britain. Israel had no choice but to deliver the devastating blows throughout the Middle East in order to protect themselves from being under the threat of complete extinction for the second time in the past one hundred years. The devastation throughout the world was now drawing millions of bible believing Christians as well as millions of Torah believing Jews not to mention millions of Koran believing Moslems into preaching that end of the world was here. The horror of the end of the world was making a lot of people throughout the world begin to take their religion very seriously as well as those who were previously not religious or believing that there was no god in existence were suddenly receiving their wake up calls at the worst possible moment. They were not only trying to make sense of everything, but they were also trying to get their lives in order so they can meet their heavenly maker and enter the highest places of their respective religions possible.

7:30pm

"The death toll continues to rise in the attacks throughout America as well as American interests overseas." the WBMD-TV reporter began "At least one hundred million were killed when a group believed to be al-Qaeda or an offshoot of al-Qaeda launched a multi-pronged attack against several American cities, every shopping mall in the United States, our infrastructure, mass media, governmental agencies and our military both domestic as well as overseas. No one knows the full extent of the damage that today's Black Friday attacks both short term as well as long term, but we can say that the damage that was inflicted on the United States was unprecedented."

"Why is President Grumbly doing nothing about the attacks?" Doug Downey asked Rob Bishop.

"Either President Grumbly is surveying the damage or he has something up his sleeve which is no good." Agent Bishop replied.

"I would go with the assumption that he is up to something." Ian Daley said.

"Same here," Frank Carter noted.

"Regardless of what President Grumbly is thinking." Agent Downey began as he then continued "We are all in a lot of trouble because of the extent of the attack. No one knows if our military equipment is in working order so we can retaliate. No one is investigating whether al-Qaeda or someone else carried out the attacks besides us. This says a lot for the state that this country is in at this hour. I am beginning to believe that President Grumbly may be up to something."

"Also the death tolls are increasing in both Great Britain as well as Israel. In Great Britain at this hour there are twenty million people who were killed with scores more wounded. Also there is a civil war continuing in Great Britain as well with British citizens fighting Moslems throughout the country. Also the rescue operations are well underway in cities such as London, Liverpool, Manchester and Glasgow to name a few. Hazmat units are entering these cities as well as other cities and towns throughout the English nation. It may take at least several days though for the Hazmat operations to actually begin in earnest given the fact there are not enough hazmat workers to enter each city. This has caused around the clock training for volunteers Right now the Red Cross workers in Great Britain are feeling very taxed as their resources have been completely stretched given the devastation throughout England as a result of the attacks that took place at seven o'clock London time." he then paused and continued on "In Israel, Tel Aviv, Haifa, Jaffa and several other cities and villages have been decimated as a result of the attacks. However the Israeli government has escaped decapitation and is located in undisclosed locations throughout Israel at this very hour. Right now, Israelis and Palestinians are fighting one another throughout Israel while Armies of Arab citizens in other Middle Eastern countries are converging upon Israel in order to join in on the battle. At least a million Israelis were killed while countless others have been wounded as a result of the attacks. We are also receiving reports of casualties throughout the Middle East as a result of the nuclear exchange that took place almost four hours ago. Jordan has at least a million dead and scores who were injured as a result of the nuclear exchange. In Syria, less than a million have been killed with millions more wounded during the nuclear exchange. In Lebanon, three fourths of the nation were either badly wounded or killed. The death toll in Lebanon has yet to be made official, but there are indications that more than one half of the Lebanese citizens perished in the nuclear exchange while the Lebanese government is hanging on by a thread. In Iraq, two million killed, and at least five million were wounded. In Iran three million were killed and another ten million were wounded while Iran is now in complete anarchy when its government was decapitated during the nuclear strikes and the American response to their warships being nuked by the Iranian silkworm missiles that were fired upon them within the past four hours. In Saudi Arabia, two and a half million people were killed and another seven million were killed during the nuclear strikes that have completely destroyed Mecca, Median and Riyadh. The Grand

Mosque in Mecca has been completely destroyed and as a result every Moslem is now in the process of making their way to Israel in order to retaliate against the Israelis as well as their government because of the attack against the heart of the Moslem religion. The Saudi government has been completely decapitated as well during the retaliation strike by Israel. In Afghanistan six million were killed and another ten million were wounded as a result of the attacks. In fact there will be questions about whether the al-Qaeda leadership was killed as a result of the nuclear strikes throughout the Middle East that took place only four hours ago. We are now receiving reports that China has bombed Taiwan especially the capital Taipei where we are receiving unconfirmed reports that the entire government of Taiwan has been decapitated. The Chinese military has as of right now begun its invasion of Taiwan. North Korea has attacked both South Korea and Tokyo with its Taepodong VII missiles as South Korean President Choi was killed as well as the entire delegation for the Pacific Rim Trade conference. The North Koreans have begun its bombing campaign of its neighbor to the south while beginning a full scale invasion of South Korea. As the non-stop coverage of the 11/23 attacks as well as the subsequent retaliatory strikes were still continuing on at this very hour only five and a half hours after it began. An entire world was now riveted to the incessant coverage of the most devastating terrorist attacks in the history of the world." the CNN reporter then paused as he was handed a slip of paper. He quickly glanced at it and then muttered "This can't be?"

"Yes it is." the person handing him the slip of paper replied "Just read it from the teleprompter." she then added. The reporter now looked at the camera and began "Just when the nightmarish events of today were not enough, there are now reports of additional missiles that have been fired from North Korea as well as China. They have landed in Tokyo, Alaska, Hawaii, California, Oregon and Washington. It is becoming very obvious that what began as a strike by al-Qaeda has become a diabolical multinational attack that is still being carried out against the United States and its allies."

"I wonder how much more far reaching this could get?" Frank Carter mused aloud.

"I have no question that these developments may not be the last." Ian Daley replied "I shudder to think what will occur next."

"What do you think will occur next?" Agent Bishop inquired.

"I hate to think that this may become President Grumbly may have had a hand in this." Daley stated.

"I wouldn't be surprised if that was the case." Carter noted "I have seen the man in action on numerous occasions. He is perfectly capable of doing something like this."

"But why?" Agent Downey inquired "Why aid al-Qaeda? There has to be other accomplices domestically."

"I think we can rule out that he was an unwilling pawn in today's attacks." Agent Bishop began "Look how he is taking his time forming a cabinet. I am sure that if any one of us were in Grumbly's shoes that we would have formed a cabinet by now not to mention taken more action than what has been taken to this point."

"That is exactly why I have long felt that Grumbly is in on the attacks." Daley added as the four remained transfixed by the ongoing coverage of the attacks.

"What happened here?" Tim Lake began as he saw the security cameras inside the security room at the Galleria Mall. He saw that the computer was smashed and they had no luck with the screening. The computer technician was now searching to see if there were any backup files present. For a little while there were none until he stumbled upon one. He then said to Lake "I found what we were looking for. I will need to rewire the cameras onto the system. Soon we will have everything up and running again. We'll find out the identities of those who carried this out."

"Can you do me one other favor?" Lake then asked.

"Anything." the computer technician began "What would it be?"

"We need to go with the assumption that it may not only be al-Qaeda who carried out this diabolical attack."Tim began "I think they may have had some help if you know exactly what I mean."

"I think I know exactly what you mean." he started "Would you consider anyone who worked in this mall a suspect?"

"I refuse to rule anyone who worked here out." Lake noted.

"Israel is now a complete battlefield." began the CNN reporter who was now giving live stream coverage through night camera lens. He was able to zoom in at a great distance from a mountainous area outside Hebron, Israel. "As you can see from a distance, the fire from the guns as well as machine guns what seems to have become one huge battlefield. You can not only fires, but lights from the gunfire as well as the machine gunfire from the weapons that are being used throughout Israel at this very late hour in the evening. Everyone is very riled up and the adrenaline is beyond pumped up for every person who is participating in this very historically large scale all-out battle in which everything has been put on the line for Israel, the Palestinian people as well as the rest of the Arab world for that matter. There is a passage in the bible in which the final battle of the world will take place at Armageddon. In this case we are live at the exact site in which Armageddon will take place here in Har Megiddo. It is ironic about what was first mentioned in the bible from up to three thousand and five hundred years ago may very well be actually playing out right before our own very eyes at this very hour." As the live stream coverage through the CNN website was still ongoing. Only those whose internet coverage was not affected by the attacks were watching the live non-stop coverage of what millions upon millions of people were beginning to believe was in fact the final battle that would ever take place in the history of the world. Meanwhile those who were now transfixed by the battle were now waiting to see if Jesus, the Mahdi or the Twelfth Imam would show up at the battle depending on what religion that the person who was watching the live battle throughout Israel believed in. Just then there were now explosions that rocked the area to the extent that the live stream was suddenly finished.

"What happened?" Agent Bishop asked.

"I think there may have been another nuclear strike if I didn't know any better." Ian Daley replied as he then added "I think that it is most likely that the internet stream was knocked out due to the severity of the explosions.

"Whatever it is." Agent Downey began "It has made me become a very religious person."

"Everything that has happened today has made me reevaluate everything I have ever done in my life." Frank Carter began "I was raised to be a very devout Catholic and all these born again Christians have been preaching incessantly to me throughout my life that Roman Catholicism was in fact a cult and not the true way to Jesus. For years I thought that they were a cult. However with this final battle taking place at Har Megiddo I am beginning to think that they were right."

"With all due respect there are some signs that have yet to take place even before that battle is to take place. Among them would be the rapture in which millions of believers are to be raptured into heaven without dying. There has to be a one world nation which is to be led by the Antichrist. It is the Antichrist who must reign for seven years before that final battle is to take place. At first he will be like a lamb who among all things will sign a treaty with Israel. Halfway through the Antichrist's seven year reign, he will be killed suddenly and then rise again proclaiming that he is god and everyone must worship him. He will kill the two witnesses who have been preaching against the Antichrist for years while turning against Israel and resuming hostilities against the Jewish State. He will kill millions upon millions of people who will refuse to worship him. Then all of those who refuse to worship the antichrist will flee to a mountain in Israel and remain there until the final battle at Har Megiddo which is also known as Armageddon. There Jesus will return along with his legions of saints and angels. They will eliminate the anti-Christ as well as the forces of evil. Once this victory is achieved Jesus will reign for a thousand years in the New Jerusalem while the devil is tied up and thrown into the abyss. After the one thousand year period is over, the devil will then be freed and he will unleash his final havoc among the people. In the end the Devil will be killed and will no longer be a threat to anyone. This is how the end of the world will take place." Agent Bishop preached to his friends while trying to reassure them that the end of the world was not yet upon them and that there were signs that had to occur before the end of the world would take place.

"Are you a Christian?" Ian Daley asked Bishop.

"Yes." Bishop replied "I have been saved since I was seven." Bishop replied.

"In that case I wish to accept Jesus Christ as my savior." Daley replied.

"So would I." the others stated.

The citizens of Formosa Island were now witnessing Chinese troops stationed throughout their land. Many of the citizens had went to bed only hours earlier to a world which had dramatically changed within the past five and a half hours. Not only were they reeling over the news that they were conquered by China, but of the battle in North Korea, the attacks in the United States and Great Britain as well as Israel. They were now learning for the first time of the all-out war throughout the Middle East. They were quickly realizing that this was one huge plot that had unfolded in the past few hours.

At the same time in North Korea, the citizens there were digging in the underground bunker and they found a few more bodies. They were able to quickly identify them as the leadership of the North Korean government. Among the dead was King Jung. The rescue workers began to cheer and dance among themselves. They quickly understood that the permanent reunification of the two Koreas would finally take place.

9:00pm

"Ian." Chief of Staff Roberts began "It's me Kirk "I am afraid that we may have a serious problem."

"What's going on?" Daley asked Roberts.

"I'm concerned about the president." Roberts began.

"How so?" Ian inquired.

"I'm afraid that he has been dragging his feet in investigating the matter. He has been on his phone talking to people rather than beginning to retaliate as well as rebuild America." Kirk stated.

"For all practical purposes, the president could be trying to get a hold of people who could help him rebuild this country." Daley suggested.

"I think it's more than that." Roberts noted.

"What do you mean by that?" Ian mused aloud.

"I think he's up to something." Kirk said.

"I wonder what it could be." Daley wondered.

"That's where I need your help." Roberts started "I need you to tap into his phone."

"I wish I could, but the equipment that is required to do so was destroyed in the attacks." Ian stated.

"Then what do we do in that case?" Kirk panicked.

"Leave it to me, I will figure out something." Daley said reassuring Roberts.

"Who was it?" Frank Carter asked Ian Daley.

"That was Kirk Roberts, President Grumbly's chief of staff." Ian began "It looks like our friend has been very slow in getting the ball rolling."

"How slow?" Carter then asked.

"A snail is going at hyper speed compared the president." Daley noted.

"Are you thinking what I'm thinking?" Agent Bishop asked everyone in the room.

"I hope that what I'm thinking is not what you're thinking." Agent Downey replied.

"It seems that way to me." Ian Daley said chiming in.

"I'm afraid that we have a completely new ballgame." Carter acknowledged as the four now glanced at the local news coverage of the 11/23 terrorist attacks.

"The death toll is now up to one hundred million with at least at least another hundred and fifty million injured." the reporter for the WCBS station in Bethesda, Maryland began as she then continued "Unprecedented devastation in several cities as well as countless communities took place at two pm Eastern today. The United States government was virtually decapitated and the military was seriously crippled in the attacks. President Grumbly will address the nation at ten pm eastern with the latest on the attacks."

"Don't hold your breath Ma'am." Frank Carter began "He not going to say anything new. In fact I would be stunned if he did one thing to help this country right now." Meanwhile, there was a knock on the door. Agent Bishop drew his gun and began to walk to the door with Agent Downey following closely behind. Bishop slowly opened the door and saw a man standing there terrified at the sight of two men with their guns pointed at him. "How can we help you?" Bishop asked.

"I have a tip for you." the man replied. He was 5'7" and was of slender build. He was in his fifties and was dressed casually in a brown leather jacket and tan slacks.

"Come on in." Agent Bishop ordered as he then frisked the man "What is your name?"

"Martin Hayes." he replied "I managed the Freeman campaign."

"What do you have for us Mr. Hayes?" Bishop inquired.

"We have had a private investigator trail one of our campaign workers." Hayes began "He had been friends with a number of suspicious individuals within the lobbyist community. Those lobbyists were key contributors for the re-elect Wolcott campaign."

"I see." Bishop began.

"At least one of the lobbyists had connection to Cypress." Hayes continued in reference to Cyber Express which was a company that produced internet equipment. "Cypress helped produce the voting machines that were used in the disputed states almost three weeks ago."

"Excuse us." Agent Bishop began. He and the other three then walked over to a corner and began to speak among themselves. "Why would the a lobbyist for the Democratic

Party use voting machines that have been rigged in order to favor a Republican candidate in the states where the ballots are disputed?"

"Something doesn't ring true." Agent Downey replied.

"I know someone who is high up in the Freeman campaign. Please let me speak to him first before anything is done." Daley implored.

"Let him." Frank Carter began "Ian, I would like to come along with you. If this is what I think it is, we could have a scandal unlike anything this country has ever experienced or any other country for that matter."

The citizens of the country that was previously known as Taiwan until hours earlier were huddled inside their homes while sending text messages to one another debating about whether to revolt against China. They were feeling not only a collective uncertainness but a collective fear at the same time. Meanwhile one particular conversation was unfolding between two former Taiwanese military officials which quickly became very animated.

"We need to get our top scientists together and create some sort of super virus which will cripple the mainland and then we can take out their nukes as well as other weaponry." Heop Soi Wen the former colonel of the Taiwanese military stated via text message.

"We would likely need to recruit another country to help us out and the United States would not be the best option right now given how devastating the attack was for them . . ." Sang Chop Le the former admiral noted as he sent his reply to Wen.

"I am convinced that the only reason we were invaded and conquered was because the United States was crippled yesterday." Wen stated as he fired off another text message to Le "Besides I think we should seriously consider recruiting India if anyone for this task."

"I cannot think of a more appropriate country at this stage of the game than India. They will likely deny our request, but if we get a multinational coalition going then we would stand a much better chance. We need to involve the United States, Israel and Great Britain in some manner since they were attacked as well." Le added.

"You know that we would not only be fighting China, but very likely the entire Middle East as well as the Moslems worldwide at the same time." Wen acknowledged "We are going to be in for quite an uphill battle, but it is one we must fight for the sake of humanity."

"I am concerned about Russia." Le began "They have been very quiet throughout this whole crisis. I am certain that they are up to something. I don't know to what extent they are involved in this, but it is very clear that we cannot trust them especially at this time."

"I am becoming quite convinced that they are playing the role of a sleeping giant in this crisis." Wen noted.

"Try playing the part of a sleeper nation." Le suggested "They are likely waiting for their cue to enter this conflict."

"I completely agree with you." Wen added as the conversation quickly came to a dead end for a little while.

"Who do we send in for the reunification meeting?" a former North Korean governmental who was wrongfully dismissed from his post years ago by Kim Jong Il inquired.

"You would be the leader of such a group." An opposition leader to the now former North Korean dictatorship inquired "I would also be part of such a delegation. I know a few of the leaders of the other opposition groups. I can get them together and they can bring any other leaders of the other opposition groups to a meeting that can be held as soon as a few hours from now."

"Get them together." Tam Un Jin began as the former government official continued "Timing is of the essence. We cannot have a nation such as Russia or China take advantage of the power vacuum and take over our land. We endured one dictatorship; we refuse to be subjected to another one." With that Su Han Soo left and began to gather the leaders of the opposition groups together for the emergency meeting.

"Why haven't the North Koreans approached us for a reunification meeting?" asked the South Korean Defense Secretary Foo who was their acting president.

"I think they are trying to gather together a delegation in order to discuss reunification." Foo's assistant Wong replied "They are so disorganized that this could take a while."

"Remember how we thought our brothers in the north would put up quite a fight against us?" Foo began "I think they can quickly get a delegation together." as his secretary entered the bunker and said "You have a call from the acting Japanese prime minister.

"I will speak to him at once." Foo replied as he then took the phone from his secretary and began to speak to Acting Prime Minister Shiga "Sir, my deepest condolences about the attacks on your nation."

"Thank you." Acting Prime Minister Yorimu Shiga replied "Is this true that the entire North Korean government has been decapitated."

"Yes, that is true." Acting South Korean President Foo began "This is why I ask you to cease your bombing campaign at once."

"I will cease it for now, but if we are attacked once more we will have no choice but to resume hostilities against your nation." Shiga warned Foo "It is the pro-North Korean groups that I am concerned about."

"We are in the process of eradicating any and all threats as we speak." Foo noted.

"See that you do." Shiga stated sternly "Think about the potential consequences if you don't. Remember what we endured with Hiroshima, Nagasaki and now Tokyo as well as Kyoto, Yomouri and Hanshin."

"Prime Minister Shiga." Acting President Foo began "I understand your feeling considering what your nation has had to endure within the past seventy five years. Remember how we have suffered in the past seven hours. We lost most of our countrymen in the attacks. We respect your concerns in full."

"If you need any help in any way, please let us know. We will help you in whatever manner, shape or form that we can." Shiga offered.

"We will let you know either way Mr. Prime Minister." Foo responded.

The battle for Great Britain continued to rage on. As fighters from both sides were quickly losing their lives, the British soldiers quickly decided to resort to guerilla warfare in an attempt not only to kill more Islamic fighters, but to reduce the number of their own war casualties as well. The new style of warfare that the British soldiers chose was immediately implemented. The casualties on the Islamic side quickly began to spike. As al-Qaeda began to realize that they were losing their own soldiers very quickly, they quickly ordered their soldiers to see every private plane available and after placing explosives in each plane to crash them into every British military and governmental instillation which had yet to be attacked. Also they were ordered to crash them into large population centers and even small towns.

Neither side was winning the battle not only in Israel but Jerusalem as well. Soldiers on all sides were not gaining any ground, but they were also not losing any ground as well. Meanwhile the Israeli soldiers as well as the Jewish and Christian fighters in Jerusalem chose to adapt to the

Palestinian and Arab style of guerilla warfare as well in order to cut down on their own casualties but also to spike the casualties on the opposition at the same time. What had already become a bloodbath became even bloodier soon after. Casualties on all sides once again spiked and there was concern that the Jewish State as well as Jerusalem would quickly fall to the Palestinians, the Moslems as well as the other Arab nations who were fighting Israel.

10:00pm

"My fellow Americans." President Nate Grumbly began "The investigation into the 11/23 attacks that took place this afternoon is well underway at this hour. Due to issues regarding national security I cannot go into any detail at this time, but I can assure you that we are making some significant progress as I address you. We will rebuild as a nation and become greater than we were before today's attacks took place. The rescue and recovery of the victims of the attacks remain ongoing at this hour."

Ian Daley and Frank Carter arrived at the home of Dan Merkel. Daley knocked on the door. Markel then opened the door and gasped "Ian Daley, Frank Carter . . . what a surprise!"

"Dan, we need your help." Daley said.

"Come on gentlemen." Merkel responded "Please have a seat." The two men took a seat and Merkel then added "That attacks have been such a tragedy. We will never know the great president that Governor Freeman would have been for the American people." Merkel was 6'4" and 270 pounds. His salt and pepper combed back hair and brown eyes were now looked grim at best.

“I lost my twins today in the attack on the Galleria.” Daley replied.

“Ian, my deepest condolences.” Merkel said “They were such precious girls. They meant the world to you.”

“Thank you.’ Daley responded with a lump in his throat as his voice began to choke up with emotion.

“Dan.” Frank Carter started “Martin Hayes came to us a little while ago with some information that you had a campaign worker trailed due to suspicious activity. Is this true?”

“We have been suspicious about the activities of one of staffers towards since late-September.” Merkel began

“Activities?” Daley snapped as he cut in on the conversation “As in more than one activity?’

“That would be correct.” Merkel said.

“You know that this changes everything.” Carter stated

“How so?” Merkel mused.

“We will let you know when the conversation is over.” Carter noted “Please proceed.”

“We had to hire a private detective to trail Gary Barton. He has been keeping company with some suspicious characters. One was a known lobbyist with connections to the president and another person who has been on the government’s terrorist watch list for quite a while.” Daley noted “Wasn’t Barton was among those who inspected the voting machines in Florida before the election.”

“When did Barton inspect the voting machines?” Carter asked.

“Late last month. We had someone trail him. That person inspected the machines at the same time.” Merkel added.

"Who was the person that traveled with Barton?" Daley asked.

"Ryan Kilpatrick." Merkel noted "Yes. Why?"

"There are a number of prominent Democrats who are connected to the company." Frank Carter replied "We need to interview both Barton and Kilpatrick."

"By all means." Merkel noted as he then inquired "That thing that you were going to tell me. What is it?"

"Given the implications for national security, we will need you to come with us." Daley suggested.

"Am I in any trouble over this?" Merkel asked.

"Just the opposite." Ian started "We need to protect you from anyone who may try to knock you off over what you have verified to us. We are protecting Hayes as well." With that the three men for the safe house that was outside Bethesda.

"Mr. President," began Chief of Staff Kirk Roberts "I need to have a word with you."

"Kirk, give me a moment please." President Grumbly said. He then continued on with his conversation. "Is it a deal?'

"Yes." the voice on the other end replied "We have a deal." as the person then hung up the phone. Grumbly then placed another call. He then began to say "How is the arsenal working?" he inquired in reference to the nuclear weapons.

"That is much better than I thought. Prepare them for immediate use." President Grumbly ordered as he hung up the phone.

"Mr. President." Roberts began "How can you issue a nuclear order without the Nuclear Football present." Grumbly's chief of staff inquired knowing that the Nuclear Football was a briefcase with the instructions for a nuclear strike inside. Grumbly now stopped cold in his tracks unsure of what he would say next. Roberts then glared at the president and walked out of the room. As Roberts began to cool off, he began to mull over his options. Kirk knew that there was only one real option to take. He then returned five minutes later and said "I am tendering my resignation effective immediately."

"Why, Kirk?" President Grimes inquired.

"I am fed up with your inactivity when it comes to managing this crisis." Roberts shot back.

"Kirk, you don't understand the magnitude of the attacks. We have been for all practical purposes devastated in every area possible. I am doing everything in my power to get this nation back on track." Grumbly bellowed.

"At least I would do everything I can. You have yet to even begin to do a thing." Roberts noted as he walked out of the room.

Tim Lake was now taking a break from the investigation at the Galleria Mall. He walked outside into the crisp cold air that was hanging below. The skies were clear to the extent where you could not only see the moon, but one could count the stars that were in the sky. Lake then placed a call to Ian Daley. Daley picked it up and said "How can I help you Tim?"

"I'm worried about you." Lake replied.

"Thanks. I'm worried about me as well." Daley began "Is there anything new in the investigation?" Ian then asked.

"The terrorists took advantage of a secluded parking lot in order to enter the mall undetected." Tim started "They did some shopping and returned to the car. We were able to catch footage of them when they first entered the mall and then after they left and returned once more. They did not have their suicide vests on the first time. They returned looking bulkier and they even had different shopping bags. It was in those bags that they carried their weapons in. Have you or your team been able to find out anything?"

"We may have discovered a domestic link to the attacks." Daley began "I need you to look into the backgrounds of your employees. I think someone deliberately missed something. That in turn led to what happened today."

"I will look into it right away." Tim responded "How far reaching could the domestic link become?" he then asked.

"It could very well lead to President Grumbly." Ian acknowledged "Please keep it quiet though. I don't want this to get out yet."

"You have my word." Lake said as he went to his desk and began to conduct background checks on his security guards.

The casualties continued to spike on all sides in Israel, especially in Jerusalem. The Israeli military quickly made the decision to bomb the Palestinian and Arab soldiers wherever they gathered. Meanwhile the Christian extremist soldiers were quickly becoming neutralized to the extent where they could no longer put up a fight. They proceeded to back down and instead fight on the side of the Jews in order to increase their chances of survival so they could regroup and fight once again in the future. Meanwhile the Israeli military was now beginning to quickly take down the opposition. Cluster after cluster of Palestinian as well as Arab soldiers were being killed. As this was occurring, the Israelis were slowly beginning to get the upper hand in the conflict.

The first wave of small private planes began to crash into the British military instillations as well as the population centers. Once the Royal Air Force realized this they ordered the fighter jets which survived the initial attacks to shoot down any private plane that was flying in Great Britain as well as any plane which even flew into British airspace since the flight ban to, from and inside Great Britain was already in effect. One by one the Royal Air Force began to shoot down the planes. Although some of them continued to crash into their targets, the majority of them were shot down. Meanwhile, the Royal Air Force proceeded to begin to bomb the cluster of al-Qaeda soldiers who were fighting the British soldiers. With that the al-Qaeda soldiers were quickly being killed and threat to the British soldiers was now beginning to decrease by the second. For the first time since the conflict began, Great Britain was beginning to get the upper hand in the war with the Moslem extremists. They were now hoping that the newfound momentum would lead them directly to victory although it would be one that would be achieved at a very high price.

"How are you coming along?" Tam Un Jin asked Su Han Soo.

"Everyone is on board so far." Soo began "In fact there are a number of splinter groups who we didn't know were in existence until now. Most of them are already on board. It's the leaders of the groups we have let to find that we must extend our offer to."

"Please let me know as soon as you find out from them. I must inform President Foo of the latest developments." Jin replied as he ended the first call and quickly placed a second to President Foo. Foo quickly answered the phone and replied "Tam Un Jin, it has been ages since we last spoke. How can I help you?" Foo had recruited Jin as a spy years earlier.

"We are gathering together a delegation consisting of opposition leaders to the now former dictatorship. Everyone who we have had contact with so far is on board. We are trying to locate a few more opposition groups who were previously unknown to us. I am certain that they will join my delegation as well."

"Once they join, please call me again so we can set up the reunification talks. Also, this brings me to another topic I wish to speak to you about. I spoke to the acting Japanese Prime Minister Shiga. He is concerned that groups who were sympathetic to your dictatorship may try to launch a series of attacks. Not only against us, but Japan as well. If Japan is attacked, Prime Minister Shiga will have no alternative but to retaliate immediately and with full force. That is why it is important that you help us eradicate any groups who are sympathetic to the former dictatorship before it is too late." Foo stated.

"Consider it done." Jin responded.

"We need to let our contacts in the other nations know." Col. Wen suggested to Admiral Le via text.

"I have a number of contacts myself." Admiral Le noted as he fired off a text message to his old comrade.

"However we do this we must be discrete not to mention very careful. For all we know the mainland may have already put a wiretap on or even bugged our phones for that matter." Wen mused "If they haven't they will soon enough."

"We definitely need to put out feelers to the Indians, the Britons as well as the Japanese, the North Koreans, the Israelis and the Americans." Le noted.

"That must be done immediately." Wen noted as he added "We will both send out inquiries to our contacts at once." With that the conversation ended and they began to reach out to their military as well as political contacts and those in the intelligence communities in the aforementioned nations. The men began to send text massages to each contact in order to avoid being detected by the Chinese government as well as the Chinese intelligence agencies. The waiting game was now in full swing.

11:00pm

"As of right now." the WBMD reporter began as he gave the hourly update on the television "The death toll from today's terrorist attacks has now risen to one hundred and thirty million with another one hundred and fifty million injured. There has been no official claim of responsibility although it is obvious that al-Qaeda carried out today's 11/23 attacks. Meanwhile rumors have been rampant that al-Qaeda may have had help from a foreign government presumably China or Russia although officials from both countries have denied being involved in the plotting or carrying out of the attacks. As the United States is on edge that more attacks may occur especially tonight, President Grumbly's seemingly inactive stance since he was sworn in has resulted in the growing impatience of the American people who demand action immediately. Millions of Americans are taking to the streets at this hour either looting and rioting or demanding that either the government takes action and fast or the people will do so themselves. The growing threat of anarchy throughout the United States is too hard to ignore. It could happen as soon as tonight or it could happen by tomorrow morning.

"How much more can we wait before we take action ourselves?" a young man began as he continued on "We are at the tipping point of this crisis and the president is not doing a thing to help us. We need a real president. One who can lead this country."

"We need President Grumbly to step aside since he is not protecting this country nor is he helping us for that matter." a middle aged women shot back "What is he waiting for, for us to be conquered by the terrorists?" she blurted.

"I think we need to understand the full extent of how badly we were attacked. I am confident that the president is trying to find out who survived in order to put together a government while checking to see how badly the military equipment and weaponry were damaged as well. We need to go into this latest phase of the War on Terror with a backup group of governmental officials as well as full weaponry and equipment in order to defeat al-Qaeda once and for all!" a third person who happened to be a retired Army general noted.

"These are some of the reactions tonight."

"What did you find out?" Agent Bishop asked Ian Daley.

"I spoke to my contact inside the Freeman campaign. There were able to verify that they were suspicious about one of their staffers towards the end of the campaign." Daley began as Agent Dawson cut him off "What on earth does that have to do with the attacks?"

"They hired a private detective to trail him. He had been keeping company with some suspicious characters. One was a known lobbyist with connections to the president and another person who has been on the government's terrorist watch list for quite a while." Daley noted "The same person had been among those who inspected the voting machines in Florida before the election."

"Wasn't Cypress the company that made the voting machines?" Agent Downey mused aloud.

"Yes. Why?" Daley asked wondering what the response was going to be.

"There are a number of prominent Democrats who are connected to the company." Agent Downey replied "And guess who's among them? President Grumbly."

"If that's the case then why didn't they rig the election in their favor?" Agent Daley began as he quickly added "And why was Grumbly out of town during the attacks? Are you thinking what I'm thinking?"

"President Grumbly is in on the attacks." Bishop replied.

"Also, President Grumbly and the late President Wolcott always hated each other." Daley noted "We need to hunt both Grumbly and Briggs down at once!"

Tim Lake was in the process of carrying out a background check on the director of the Galleria Mall security. Lake Googled his name and then saw a lot of entries with his name. He scrolled down each entry until he saw contributors to Congressman Nate Grumbly's most recent campaign.

Grumbly saw how much the late director contributed and he broke out in a cold sweat. Tim then logged onto the mall's email accounts. He then logged into the late director's account and began to read the emails from the most recent until the latest one. He quickly stumbled upon the one that was dated for this morning at 5:45am

> Carl,
>
> Wait for my text to find out when to take your lunch break today.

Lake then instinctively walked over to the evidence truck that was outside the Galleria Mall. He saw the person who was cataloging the evidence. "I need to look at the cellphone of the director of Mall Security. I think there may be a breakthrough."

"Let me get it for you." he replied. Within moments he got the phone and handed it to Lake. Lake now turned on the phone and pressed the button that said messages. Tim quickly found the message to Carl Quinn which said "Carl, you and your crew can take your lunch around 1:30pm." The text was send at 9:50am just seconds after the Ohio Secretary of State Eric Watson was gunned down. He recalled that the director was in the office watching Fox News at the time of the shooting. He had sent a text right after the shooting. "So this is why he didn't prepare for a contingency plan should a massacre like this occur. He knew that one was going to take place all along." Lake screamed while he was unable to contain his rage. Lake took a picture of the text and then sent it to Ian Daley. Tim then called Ian. Daley picked it up and said "What is it Tim? I was about to ready your text message."

"I need you to look at it and then I will explain to you why I sent it to you." Lake replied.

"You mean that your mall director and a worker were involved in the attack." Ian surmised.

"That would be correct." Tim began "I saw the director send a text message right after the shooting. That was why there was no one attending the camera from one thirty to two thirty this afternoon."

"This explains a lot." Daley began as he then added "I am afraid that the plot is a lot mare far reaching than what I had previously thought. I am certain that there is a direct correlation between the recount and the attacks."

"How so?" Lake inquired. With that Daley explained everything to Lake. Lake then ended the call feeling a state of shock that he had never before experienced in his life and one that he hoped that he would never ever experience once again.

"Have you had any responses?" Colonel Wen asked Admiral Le via text message.

"Nothing yet." Le replied.

"Keep trying." Wen added as both cell phones quickly received an avalanche of replies. They both looked at each response and they quickly learned that everyone they contacted said that they would help out Wen and Le liberate Taiwan.

Tam Un Jin now received a call from Su Han Soo. Soo began the conversation feeling very upbeat. He knew that from this point on that the day if not the days, weeks, moths and even years would become a lot better than they previously were.

"I spoke to the rest of the opposition groups." Soo began "They wish to know how soon the meeting with you is to take place."

"Immediately. We will meet as soon as everyone arrives at Hapeo." Jin replied. Hapeo is a very small village in the middle of North Korea.

"I will let them know at once." Soo noted. As the conversation came to a quick end, Jin placed another call. This time it was to South Korean President Foo. "President Foo, the delegation will meet within hours from now. That is as soon as everyone arrives at Hapeo." Jin stated.

"How are you coming along at eradicating the opposition groups?" Foo then inquired.

"My men are in the process of eliminating them as we speak." Jin responded.

"That I am glad to hear. I will update Prime Minister Shiga at once." President Foo said. He then placed a call to inform Prime Minister Shiga. "Sir, the North Koreans are in the process of eradicating the pro-dictatorship groups as we speak. They have our full cooperation."

"I am so relieved that we have your full cooperation." Shiga proclaimed.

"It is the former North Koreans who are cooperating with us. I was concerned that there may have been some opposition though." Foo added.

"Why would you think such a thing?" Shiga began "The North Koreans surrendered to you very easily."

"Although they surrendered very easily, we had a natural suspicion that there was a change that this was running a little too smoothly." Foo acknowledged "That comes from past experience."

"That much I understand. Keep up the good work and keep me posted." Shiga requested.

"We will do so on both fronts." Foo replied as the call came to an end.

For the first time since the al-Qaeda invasion of Great Britain began, al-Qaeda soldiers were beginning to retreat. Meanwhile they were also coming to the realization that they would lose the war and decided to destroy as many small towns in Great Britain as possible. They knew that they had to kill as many infidels as possible before being killed themselves. It was the killing of infidels before becoming martyrs that enticed them from the beginning. They knew that a trip to Paradise along with encountering seventy two virgins was a reward for their deeds while they were among the living that made it an incentive to wage jihad to begin with. Immediately the massacres in the small towns especially along the British countryside were well under way. In some cases, the terrorists were killed before inflicting any harm, in others cases they were killed only after inflicting much harm. With that the number of al-Qaeda fighters was now dwindling even more.

In Israel, the Arab and Palestinian armies began to pull back. They were engaging in suicide attacks against Israel towns, cities as well as military and governmental instillations. As one group of armies began to pull back, another from an Arab country began to arrive. Depending on how well organized they were they would either get off to a quick start or be defeated very rapidly. Although they were realizing their dream of following their ancestor's actions in what was becoming the modern day version of the Crusades, the results for each Islamic army was mixed. As success or disaster greeted each army, they were determined to fight to the last person knowing that Arab as well as Islamic pride hung in the balance. Meanwhile, the Israeli military was holding off the Palestinian and Arab advance as both groups of armies tried to make their way well inside Israel. They had set mine bombs to kill the opposing armies. As they fell into the trap, the advance was becoming even slower while the casualties for the Arab and Palestinian armies were increasing exponentially. Meanwhile another threat to Israel was just beginning. The Moslems from other nations especially non-Arab ones were now arriving in Israel. They flew in from Europe, Russia and Asia and landed in cities such as those which were near the Israeli border. There was now another dimension to the ongoing jihad. It was one that would ultimately either make or break Israel. The Israel government met to discuss what to do with the latest threat. They came to a very quick consensus that every Islamic, Arab and Palestinian soldier regardless of national origin had to be killed in order to save Israel from ahniliation.

11:55pm

Agents Bishop and Downey led the FBI SWAT team into the safe house where President Grumbly was residing. Ian Daley, Frank Carter and Tim Lake were among the contingent that entered the residence.

"Are we about to be under attack once again?" President Grumbly asked.

"We know everything Mr. President." Agent Downey replied "From the tampering of the voting machines right up to the Watson assassination and the attacks. We know the real reason you were out of town Mr. President and it wasn't to take care of a some personal matters." as the agents had drawn their guns on the president. President Daley now realized that the agents had cracked the case.

"Why." Ian Daley asked the soon to be former President Nate Grumbly "Why?"

"Someone had to make the Republicans look bad." Grumbly replied "Remember what happened with those chads back in 2000. There would never have been a 9/11 if those votes were counted properly."

"I lost my wife on 9/11 and my two daughters today thanks to people like you!" Daley shot back as he began to squeeze Grumbly's throat "How could you!" as two FBI agents pulled Daley off the now former acting President.

"Enough Ian!" Agent Bishop replied "We'll take it from here. Agent Downey please remove Daley from this room at once." Bishop ordered."

"Yes sir." Downey replied. He removed Ian Daley from the room. With that Bishop continued on with the interrogation. "Didn't you think that this would somehow get back to your own party?"

"You don't get it." Grumbly began "This wasn't just about weakening the Republicans. It was about weakening the Democrats as well."

"Why?" Bishop asked as there was a knock on the door of the interrogation room. "I'm busy!" Bishop replied shouting through the door.

"It's urgent!" Agent Downey bellowed "I need you right away! Something huge has just happened!'

"I'll be right out!" Bishop yelled as he stormed out of the interrogation room "What is so important that you had to interrupt my breakthrough with the scum of the world."

"You need to see what is unfolding on CNN immediately." Downey shot back "This is beyond our worst nightmare!"

"Today was our worst nightmare if I recall!" Bishop began "What can top what occurred today?" he asked half sarcastically and half seriously."

"Just watch Trust me!" Agent Downey began as the words were sputtering out of his mouth. Bishop then began to watch as his mouth dropped over what was being said.

"Today we have liberated America from your infidel leaders." Ayman al-Zawahiri began "I am now your new leader. Your President Nate Grumbly who was born Najid Fawaz was so kind to sign a treaty with us knowing that he lacked the talent to lead. America is now in a better place. America's new place is not as a superpower but under Dar el-Islam.'

"Now I hope every American rises up and fights to take back this country!" Ian Daley proclaimed.